BLOOD TRADE

BLOOD TRADE

JUDGE, JURY, & EXECUTIONER™ BOOK TWELVE

CRAIG MARTELLE
MICHAEL ANDERLE

DISRUPTIVE IMAGINATION

LMBPN Publishing
PMB 196, 2540 South Maryland Pkwy
Las Vegas, NV 89109

Version 1.00, May 2021
ebook ISBN: 978-1-64971-744-3
Print ISBN: 978-1-64971-745-0

THE BLOOD TRADE TEAM

Thanks to our Beta Readers

Micky Cocker, James Caplan, Kelly O'Donnell, and John Ashmore

Thanks to the JIT Readers

Daryl McDaniel
Zacc Pelter
Rachel Beckford
Dave Hicks
Jackey Hankard-Brodie
Thomas Ogden
James Caplan
Veronica Stephan-Miller
Micky Cocker
Dorothy Lloyd
Kelly O'Donnell
John Ashmore
Larry Omans
Peter Manis

If we've missed anyone, please let us know!

Editor

Lynne Stiegler

We can't write without those who support us
On the home front, we thank you for being there for us

We wouldn't be able to do this for a living if it weren't for our readers
We thank you for reading our books

CHAPTER ONE

Federation Base Station 11

Light eluded the corridor like it knew it was unwelcome. A couple strolled along, squinting at the plates, looking for their room, less than amused to be walking in darkness.

But the Bad Company warrior knew how to fight. The darkness should have been afraid of *him*. He pushed the female alien behind him, protecting her with his heavily muscled frame as they continued down the corridor, peering closely at panels to count the doorways until they reached theirs.

Love at first sight. The warrior spent too much time on board the *War Axe* to meet someone special, but here, on vacation, his first night on the station, he ran into Xulia selling souvenirs. He'd been mesmerized from the first moment he saw her.

And now, six hours later, they were going to get some private time. He would know by morning if she was the one for him.

"Ah-ha!" he exclaimed and held his hand in front of the access panel. Registration had done their job, and the door swished open. "Lights."

The room remained dark.

"Maybe there's a panel inside." She pushed past him into the room.

"Wait." He hurried after her, catching her in two steps and pulling her to him. The door swished closed behind him. She slid her arms around his waist and rested her head on his chest. He forgot that he stood in the darkness with his eyes closed while he ran his hands slowly up and down her back, feeling her vibrate at his touch.

The stunner snapped and arced. The female tried to push away, but the energy increased until the warrior fell, shaking and twitching.

"Watch what you're doing, dumbass!" she growled toward the corner. "Bag him and ship him out, but you better double whatever sedative you give him because he could be trouble."

"We're going to make a fortune on this one alone." The lights came on and a second alien, a male of the same species, stepped forward. He waved his arm, and two more like him came out of the bathroom carrying an antigrav stretcher. "Was he alone?"

"Like a newborn on a forest moon. Easy prey. I think we need to find out where these guys go on vacation and help ourselves to the buffet of nano-enhanced horny bastards. After a week, we'll be gone and wealthy to the point we'll never have to work again. Not bad for a couple refugee farmers from Krawlas." She folded into her conspirator's arms while the laborers secured a broadcast field dampener over the warrior's head and moved him to the stretcher.

Wyatt Earp, Keeg Station

"Don't forget to leave the ship!" Groenwyn waved over her shoulder with her free hand. She walked hand-in-hand with Lauton down the corridor toward the airlock and the ramp that led off the ship.

Magistrate Rivka Anoa watched them go, unsure if she would have time to do as Groenwyn suggested. She had work to do with the SCAMP interns if they were ever going to be turned loose. Those were self-contained artificial mobility platforms—powerful sentient intelligences riding around in android bodies.

A small bark sounded behind her. She expected to hear the nails on the deck plates and waited for it. After another warning bark, the alien dog-like creature called Tiny Man Titan—because of his weight in kilos versus his belief that he was much bigger—scrambled by, slipping and sliding as he raced toward the far end of the corridor, where the hatch to Engineering opened for him. He disappeared through it, and the hatch closed.

There was a time when Rivka had been banned from entering the engineering spaces where the Embassy of the Singularity resided because that was where Ankh, a Crenellian, kept his technology workshop.

She had gotten that fixed, and having Ankh and the Singularity on board meant her ship had access to the best technology the Federation had to offer, like cloaking, advanced weapons, advanced communications, and a small army of SI life forms. She never knew how many were on board her ship at any point in time. It ranged from eight to a dozen, with three of those incarcerated for crimes against warm-blooded species and their own code of conduct. They were put into stasis until such time as the Singularity's brightest minds could modify a sentient's programming to return the inmates to a productive life. Rehabilitation.

Rivka wondered if Ankh was in there, but she didn't have anything in particular to bring up with him, so it was best not to interrupt. Ankh loathed small talk with every fiber of his being. She didn't care for it either. There was too much to do to waste time.

She headed toward her quarters and almost ran into Clodagh Shortall, who stood with her feet wide and her fists jammed on her hips. "Promenade," the chief engineer said.

"I'd love to go shopping, but I have paperwork to catch up on."

"You have minions." Clodagh lifted one arm and pointed at the hatch. She looked too much like the Ghost of Christmas Past for Rivka's comfort.

The two faced off, Clodagh refusing to budge. Standing as straight as she was, her baby bump showed.

Rivka pointed at it. "Is he kicking yet?"

"Just a little," Clodagh replied and softened her stance.

Rivka put a hand on the bulge. The thoughts that touched her mind were pure, untainted in any way, existing of only the sensations of sound, touch, and being fed. The Magistrate reveled in the baby's unblemished mind.

A voice came to her from far away. Clodagh.

Rivka opened her eyes, not remembering closing them.

"You looked happy. Is there something we should know?" Clodagh pressed.

"A happy baby. Made me think about my own rock hard abs."

"Spill it, Magistate." Clodagh was used to Rivka not sharing what she saw in others' minds. "What did you see?"

"A pure soul, untarnished by the world. Your baby is enjoying the journey of life."

"Could you tell, boy or girl?"

"I could not. Babies don't know until we tell them. Your baby is happy, and I would say beatific. Keep doing what you are doing, for the amount of joy your baby has given me shall carry me through the day." Rivka tried to get past Clodagh, but she blocked the Magistrate's way.

"You need to get off this ship for your sanity." Clodagh subconsciously rubbed her baby bump with one hand while laying down the law with Rivka.

A wombat bounced up behind Clodagh and nearly knocked her down when she ran into one leg.

Floyd! the happy creature called. She continued running and stopped at the airlock. *Come. Take Floyd.*

"You know you have to." Clodagh crossed her arms and stood firm, unswayed by the power of the Magistrate's position.

"Maybe Tyler can take her. I really do have a mountain of work."

"Tyler intends to take her *and* you to the promenade. I need a new business casual suit if I'm going to represent you and this ship wherever we may land." Tyler Toofakre was a dentist, general medic, and Rivka's live-in boyfriend. He brought normalcy to her existence. "And before you say it, yes, you have to go. You'll be better for it. We'll all be better for it."

He tipped his head to look down his nose at her.

"Fine." She lightly stomped one foot and scowled. "Fine, but we don't take all day, and if we buy anything, we use your credit chip."

"Alas, fair maiden, your bard is a gentle soul with no means besides a twinkle in his eye and kind words, easily and well placed. I shall care for our furry family whilst you bring order to a chaotic universe by stimulating the economy most voraciously."

"What?" Clodagh mumbled.

Rivka rolled her eyes and groaned. "He's taking me on a date, and I'm paying."

"I had to sell my business, and the wages in your employ are deplorable with a capital D!" He smiled devilishly and gestured toward the airlock, where Floyd waited impatiently. "I don't think I've been paid anything, have I?"

"How would I know?" Rivka shot back. "Maybe you're paid in other ways."

"Then I am the wealthiest man ever, although that won't buy us lunch or either of us a new outfit. Who pays for the All Guns Blazing we eat?"

Rivka half-smiled and shrugged.

Clodagh shook her head. "Great. Two people with no clue about money in charge of the money."

Rivka gave in to the inevitability of it all and waved over her shoulder as she took Tyler's hand on the way to the airlock. She made cooing sounds at Floyd, who bounced in circles until the couple arrived. Then she bolted out the doors and down the ramp to the deck of the massive hangar bay. Overhead cranes and bots were scouring the outside of her ship.

"What's going on now?" she asked, looking for a foreman.

Tyler had to lean forward to drag Rivka away. "Don't worry about it. The people with a vested interest in the work live on the ship and wish no harm to *Wyatt Earp*. They won't do anything to hurt it."

"Did you already forget the intra-atmospheric Gate?" Rivka gave him the side-eye while surrendering to Tyler's tugging on her arm and letting herself be pulled toward the hatch leading to the station.

"No one died." Tyler sounded pleased with himself.

"That's a crap standard for showing how much people care about our health and well-being."

"I didn't make the rules, but we have to live with them as they're written. You're overruled here, Magistrate. This case is closed. Records are sealed. Move on. You've lost."

Rivka trooped into the station, feeling better about being off the ship. Floyd's bounces were slowing.

"Come on, little girl," Rivka said while kneeling. Floyd collapsed into her arms. They started walking again.

"You look ridiculous," Tyler noted. "Magnificently ridiculous."

"I knew this would happen," Rivka grumbled. The elevator took them to the promenade level, where they were greeted by an integrated majesty of sight and sound.

Footsteps pounded up behind them.

CHAPTER TWO

Promenade Deck, Keeg Station, Dren Cluster

"I can't believe you would sneak off without us!" Red declared. He was still in his workout gear and sweating. Lindy wore a skimpy outfit that drew looks from the strolling shoppers.

"I was kidnapped," Rivka replied. "If you could apprehend the culprit, I'll return to the ship."

"But while we're here, maybe we can treat you to lunch," Tyler offered. "The Magistrate is paying."

Lindy nodded and looked at her husband. "Sounds good to me. I'll stay, you go get a shower."

Red looked back and forth before kissing his wife, taking a sleeping Floyd, and walking away, mumbling to himself. "Always sneaking off, making my job impossible. Damn people." He looked over his shoulder to find the group still watching him. "Impossible!" he shouted.

"Well, where shall we go to eat?"

Lindy motioned toward the shops. "Stylish yet functional shoes. From all eras of fashion."

"I like the sound of that." Rivka let go of Tyler's hand and, walking side by side with Lindy, they headed into the shopping area. Tyler followed them in but then stopped.

They didn't look back. He bucked up and sat on a bench outside the shoe store that was seemingly designed for him. He was happy to be on the outside gazing in, not inside and milling about, looking at nothing that interested him.

The shop next door sold nothing but lingerie. He turned his body so he wouldn't have to look at it.

Rivka and Lindy shopped on, from the shoe store to dresses to casual wear to accessories. They saved the lingerie shop for last. Tyler bolted into the business store for menswear but didn't find anything remotely to his taste before he reappeared to encounter Lindy and the Magistrate, their arms filled with packages. Red had returned and was leaning casually against the wall.

Lindy wore a long-tailed coat that covered her workout bikini. Red eyed it skeptically.

When the group came together, Lindy was the first to speak. "I think I could hide Mabel under this."

Red's demeanor changed almost instantly, and he smiled wider. "That's my wife," he said proudly before glancing around the area like he always did, assessing threats before returning to the conversation.

"What's for lunch?" Tyler asked.

"AGB. What else?" Rivka replied.

"I hear there's a new place with exotic Torregidorian food," Tyler offered.

Rivka studied Tyler's face before reaching for his arm. He pulled away before she could touch him.

"What?" He eyed her skeptically.

"Aren't you going to help me carry this stuff?"

He held out his arms, and while she filled them, she continued. "Torregidor. The hot green women. I'm sure that's who works there. With the Harborians unleashed on society, there was a need that seems to be getting filled by those with the entrepreneurial spirit."

"Torregidor?" Red scoffed. "They're vegetarians." He waved his hand dismissively before pleading with the Magistrate. "Don't take us to a vegetarian place, Magistrate. Please?"

"Looks like you're overruled, Doctor," Rivka said.

"Maybe I can have them deliver to AGB."

"Terry Henry Walton would like the hell out of that, I'm sure." Rivka shook her head until Tyler held out his hand. She took it. He had no subterfuge in his mind, no thoughts of green-skinned women with lithe bodies. Tyler's thoughts revolved around an enticing vegetable dish with fruit highlights. "I'll talk to TH and see if we can get that dish delivered. It looks good."

"I am an open book," Tyler muttered.

"Me too, brother," Red said, glancing sidelong at Lindy before returning to scanning the crowd for threats. "Hey. We know that guy."

Sahved waved from down the promenade. He was alone, not surrounded by children as he had been the last time they'd seen him. The tall and gangly Yemilorian hurried toward them.

"I am so glad that I have seen you, the most glad I could have ever possibly been. The gladdest, clearly!" He spoke in a tumble of words.

"Good to see you, too." Rivka made a point of looking around his legs. "Did you lose somebody?"

"They have been adopted by Harborian couples—all of them. You may see the children scattered throughout the station or on ships nearby. They seemed sad and happy at the same time. It was very strange."

"Adopted?" Rivka hadn't heard anything about the disposition. She'd assumed they would be together longer to get past the trauma of their former lives.

"Yes. It is done. Very official. But, your most wondrous and supremely wonderful Magistrate, if there is any way you would be willing to demean yourself and see a remote possibility of allowing your most humble servant, Sahved, to return to *Wyatt Earp* to continue his duties? He will most attentively clean kitchens and scrub toilets."

"Why are you talking like that? You're my investigator, who took a leave of absence. You're ready to come back. Stop goofing around, and if you have any trash, retrieve it and get back on board. We might be leaving in about thirty minutes."

"Yes, your Magistrateness. I am the most pleased I could ever possibly be once again. I shall reward your welcome with praise heaped upon your short human head. Yes. Much of that. I have been on my own too long, I guess. Just the kids and me most of the time, all of the time, and more." Before the Magistrate could reply, he rushed away, nearly bowling over a group of shoppers who received his abject apology and bow.

"We're leaving in thirty minutes?" Red asked.

"No. I said we might be. I never know, but I expect we'll be in AGB, hovering near the entrance with our meals on the way while waiting for the delivery order for my husky hunk of man candy." Rivka shrugged. "I just wanted Sahved to be on board and reintegrate with the ship for when we return. Hopefully, Clevarious can break him of the Yemilorian tendency toward superlatives by the time we get back, although 'your Magistrateness' has a ring to it."

"I told you," Red said, nodding toward Tyler. "Your name is 'Man Candy.'"

"I have no comeback to that," Tyler admitted. "No words at all." He wasn't upset by the non-revelation.

Lindy spoke up. "Where are we going next, Magistrate?"

"Don't know yet. This one," she nudged Tyler with her elbow, "and Clodagh chased me off the ship before I was able to review the cases."

"You never get a choice. You get excited looking through the cases, and then Grainger gives you the hardest one."

"Hard is relative," Rivka countered.

"It's really not," Red quipped. Lindy tried to elbow him, but her arms were full of packages. She pushed them at him until he took all of them. Then she elbowed him. "What?"

Rivka ignored him. "Let's see." She removed her data pad while they entered AGB, where they received the red-carpet treatment. Terry Henry and Char waved from one of the golf simulators. Since their retirement from the Bad Company, they had been enjoying their time off. They still got involved in operations, like on Rivka's previous case in support of the Trans-Pacific Task Force.

The data pad came to life, and she fired a high-priority message to Grainger with two simple words.

Next case?

She stuffed the pad back into the inside pocket of her leather Magistrate's jacket with the scales of justice logo pinned to it. "You know what I would like?" she asked Tyler with a smile, then strolled toward the golf cage.

She waited for Char to rock a massive drive, sending the ball past Terry's. "It's all in the trunk rotation," she said. Terry scowled at the screen.

"Nice shot, Charumati!" Joseph called from the next cage, where he and Petricia were playing a different course.

"Is this what retirement looks like? The old guy getting his ass handed to him by his young wife?" Rivka pointed at both TH and Joseph.

"But she's—" TH stopped before he said too much. They knew Char was older than him by about fifty years. It made no difference. She was forever twenty-nine, and that was the hill he needed to die on—or where they'd find his corpse. "What brings you here? Tired of beating up bad guys?"

"Hanging out between cases. We needed to pick up my investigator Sahved and restock a few things." Dokken appeared. He was the sentient German Shepherd who had adopted Terry Henry Walton. Rivka scratched behind his ears. "Keeg is a nice place for that. Off the beaten track. Are you looking at moving operations to the station and ship-yard at Tyrosint?"

Terry grabbed an iron from the bag of clubs and lined up his next shot. He had a perpetual draw, and this approach shot played to his strength. He flowed the ball down the right side of the fairway. Halfway toward the green, it started turning to the left. It hit on the apron leading to the green and rolled forward and left, around the sand trap and close to the pin. He gave Char a smug look.

"If you can't drop 'em tight, you play trick shots," she said softly.

"Expanding operations. Tyrosint is a bigger station than Keeg with more potential. The shipyard has fabrication facilities comparable to Spires, but not the high-tech manufacturing. That is something we'll establish when we have enough people there to secure it. A quarter of the Harborian fleet has already transferred. I give it a year, and it'll rival our shipyard here. It'll be what Keeg used to be, a port away from everything else with no visitors."

"I see the allure. My job would be so much easier without people." Rivka tried to look unassuming.

Terry and Char glanced at each other.

"How are you doing?" Rivka asked the dog.

Very well, but there has been a distinct lack of planetary landings, being attached to this man-child. We should vacation more on planets of green and blue.

"Shh." Terry held a finger to his lips while Char focused on the ball. She played her shot, opting for a direct approach with a ball that sailed high. She cleared the sand and then some. The ball hit the back of the green and bounced out of sight.

"Oh, bother." Char stuffed her iron back into the custom bag that bore an AGB emblem and her name. TH's did, too.

Rivka's pocket vibrated. "Gotta get back to work. It's

always nice to see you guys." Rivka waved at the four players as she walked away.

"Call if you need anything, Magistrate. Anything at all." Terry meant that. He would drop whatever he was doing to help her. She had used that silver bullet more than she wanted to, but Terry thought nothing of it. He and Char helped their friends.

"Peace to you, Marshall Dillon," Joseph called. Petricia stared oddly, not getting the reference since she was hundreds of years younger than Joseph and originally from South Africa, where they didn't have the same entertainment videos. Joseph had been a vampire, a rare breed descended from the first. With improvements in nanocyte technology, his need for blood had been eliminated.

His dark past was littered with too many human corpses drained of their life blood. Petricia had never ingested human blood, having survived on animal blood until she was rescued from her vampire overlords, dark vampires known as the Forsaken. Joseph had taken her away from all that. The two were inseparable from that point forward and had followed Terry and Char to the stars.

That had done more to help Joseph heal than anything else. Terry Henry Walton had believed in him and given him a chance to be something better. TH had also beaten the crap out of him, but that had been a long time ago.

Some lessons were harder learned than others. Terry hadn't killed him when he could have. Sometimes the best second chances were covered in blood.

Rivka looked at her datapad. Grainger's reply was only two words.

Blood trade.

She opened the attachment and tried to wade through the material, but it was too fragmented. Nothing definitive to give her an idea of where to start. With a troubled look on her face, she returned to the group, which was arguing with the host about the delivery from the Torregidorian restaurant.

"You can't get delivery in here. We're a restaurant. You buy your food here."

"I told him that," Rivka said to the host. "We'll take ours to go, please."

She paid the scantily clad green woman with a swipe of her credit chip, and Tyler took the bag. She walked away with an extra swing to her hips, a radiant smile, and a wave to the AGB patrons.

Red watched intently before turning back to the customers within the bar. "She's like a Siren calling to the sailors."

"I thought…" Tyler started but stopped when Rivka shook her head and tapped the datapad in her pocket.

"We need to go back to the ship."

CHAPTER THREE

Wyatt Earp, Keeg Station, Hangar Bay

Rivka dodged the questions and hurried in front of the others while Red loomed behind her. He was unable to get to his usual position, blocking the casual public's view and protecting the Magistrate with his body.

The others rushed along behind. Red remained stymied as he carried the bags and packages Lindy had bought.

They rolled into the hangar bay, dodged the equipment surrounding _Wyatt Earp_, and bolted into the ship. Rivka took a hard right toward the cockpit, rounding the corner and heading down the port-side corridor to her quarters, which were located behind the airlock to the cargo bay that doubled as a hangar bay.

Tyler walked in behind her, depositing her purchases on the couch as she brought up her hologrid and started talking to Clevarious, the SI who ran _Wyatt Earp_.

"I'll get your lunch," Tyler told her and reached through the images to touch her on the shoulder. She stopped manipulating the screens with finger motions to take his hand and lean her cheek against it. When she let go, she returned to the screens, and Tyler headed to the galley, where Lindy had deposited the takeout boxes.

Rivka kept the two words at the very top of her holo-grid. **Blood trade**. She had only a faint idea of what that meant and searched to find the legally actionable issues behind it. People sold their blood. They'd been doing that for centuries. That wasn't illegal since old-school hospitals had to deal with a physical product versus using nanocytes and artificial bioplasma.

Nanocytes. The key to the blood desired in the trade. Not just any blood, but that with nanos from the enhanced. Most sentient creatures subject to the Federation had nanos of some kind in their blood, like the newcomers on Rorke's Drift, but those were temporary constructs to fix specific problems. They went dormant once they were finished with the repairs to their host.

Enhanced persons like Rivka and her crew were different. Their nanocytes were active and constantly looked for cell damage to repair. They kept their hosts perpetually young and healthy. As much as she wanted to think the enhanced wouldn't sell their blood, it wasn't illegal. Most enhanced had a good understanding of how their blood could be misused. Still, there were some. It was incumbent upon the ones with Pod-docs to keep away those who would use their enhancements for personal gain.

She pulled up Federation laws on the matter. Hospital products that entered the body were regulated by the Federation's Public Health Directorate. Sanity, spot-checks, regular reporting, and sampling suggested there wasn't a problem with oversight.

There it was, in the fifth document she opened. Two Bad Company warriors had disappeared. One had since been found at the bottom of a deep stairwell on board Onyx station, as if he'd fallen ten levels, through the bottom deck, and into an area where they had to cut him free. He had no memory of what had happened. The assumption was that both were related to the blood trade.

"Don't people go AWOL on occasion? The Bad Company maintains a brutal deployment pace," she muttered before making a note to do an external evaluation of the mental health of the other warriors. "Discount the obvious before jumping to conclusions," she reminded herself.

The Magistrate leaned back in her chair and crossed her arms. With Grainger's attached documentation open on her screens, she saw too much speculation, no facts, and no causal link between the disappearances and the blood trade.

"Get me Grainger, please," she told Clevarious.

The comm screen appeared at eye-level of the grid.

The screen went dark, and a muffled voice grumbled, "What?"

"You just sent me a message a half-hour ago. How are you asleep already?"

"Rivka. Who else would interrupt when I'm sleeping like a dead man? I get so little sleep as it is, when I do get to lie down, I don't waste time. I've only been asleep for a half-hour? No wonder I feel like shit. Did you want something?"

"The blood trade. I don't see any causal links to the two

disappearances or any relation to other enhanced disappearances."

"Too many in too short a time. Find out who is kidnapping these people to sell their blood."

"I don't see anything that crosses the chasm from people disappearing to landing at the feet of the illicit blood trade. Let the Public Health Directorate handle it."

"No. Lance Reynolds personally asked for this to be handled by the Magistrates."

"I just saw TH, and he didn't say anything about it."

"He's retired. Talk to Christina, but you'll want to talk with Joseph and Petricia, too."

"They were there, too. I'll go talk with them. Thanks, Grainger." She signed off before he could give her more grief about interrupting his sleep. "Clevarious, didn't we talk about not interrupting Grainger? Aren't you talking with Beau?" Beau was the Enhanced Intelligence who ran Grainger's ship.

"I sensed your urgency, which meant that it was important enough to interrupt Grainger. It's the price of being the boss."

"But no one interrupts me," Rivka replied.

"You have better people working for you," Clevarious deadpanned.

Rivka laughed and dropped the hologrid. She reached for her Magistrate's jacket, only to find that she hadn't taken it off, then pushed the door open and almost knocked the plates out of Tyler's hand.

She grabbed two slices off hers, folded them, and ate while she walked. "Going to see TH," she mumbled through a mouthful of hot pizza.

"She's leaving again," Tyler shouted. Rivka briefly hesitated before continuing on her way. Red burst through the galley door and slammed into the Magistrate. Her remaining slices were plastered against the wall.

"I thought you were supposed to protect me?" She stared at him.

"I'm protecting you from yourself." He stood tall, puffing out his chest.

"Pie me." She held out her hand, and Tyler gave her two more slices. "We have to talk with TH and Joseph."

"Weren't we just there?" Red shook his head before leaning back into the galley. "Plates in the fridge. We're on the job."

Red slow-walked ahead of Rivka, blocking her from getting past him while stalling until Lindy could join them. She popped out of the galley, still wearing her long coat over her revealing workout gear.

"You should let your wife wear more clothes," Rivka remarked.

Red threw his hands up as his eyes shot wide. "I do *not* tell my wife what to wear!"

Rivka looked over her shoulder at Lindy. The bodyguard winked.

"You two deserve each other. Now let's get back to AGB." They hurried off the ship.

"You could use your chip to contact them," Red suggested.

"Then they'd worry for no reason. I'd much rather talk with them straight up."

"Is that the touch thing? You don't want to give anyone time to shield their thoughts from you?"

"Maybe. Don't give a suspect time to concoct a story, although TH isn't a suspect. Some habits are hard to break."

Red held out his arm, and Rivka shoved her hand behind her back. "Like I want to see your food-lust thoughts."

"I'm still hungry," he said while looking left, right, up, and down, assessing, conducting an instant risk analysis. Lindy brought up the rear with attentiveness equal to Red's. "You're not going to die on my watch."

Rivka didn't argue. She was wanted by hardcore criminals whose empires were at risk while she was alive. They had tendrils in the most unlikely places. She'd stopped taking anything for granted after Red got shot on Zaxxon Major.

In AGB, they found TH, Char, Joseph, and Petricia at the bar, sipping drinks and telling lies.

When she approached, Terry Henry was instantly wary. "What?" He sounded suspiciously like Grainger.

"How did the round go? Who won?" she asked innocently.

"We compete only against ourselves to do better with each round, gratified by the artificial outdoors."

"Char, then. Good job, sister." Rivka clenched her fist before her chest in solidarity with Charumati.

The four waited.

"You people are no fun. Of course I'm here for a reason. What can you tell me about the blood trade?"

Terry Henry's face fell, and his eyes focused so hard that Rivka thought he was staring into her soul. "That's a hard subject." He closed his eyes and groaned. "Don't tell me..."

Char blew out a long breath while resting her hand on Terry's arm.

"We might be able to provide some perspective," Joseph said barely above a whisper. "We were milked of our life blood for nearly a decade. Only our nanos kept us alive."

Rivka gasped. "A decade? What the hell do they do with the blood?"

"Rich people buy it and get most of the effect of being enhanced without getting into a Pod-doc." Joseph's voice was still soft. Petricia stared at the floor.

"Grainger thinks they're out here. Did you know there are two Bad Company warriors who've gone missing?"

"No…" TH lamented, drawing out the word. "I better call Christina."

"She was the one who reported the absences to Nathan and the General."

"She wasn't with us when we survived the attack on Joseph and Petricia. It isn't as personal an issue with her."

Rivka studied the distraught group before her while Red and Lindy kept their distance. "Is it better or worse as a personal issue?"

"It makes me cringe, thinking about what they might be going through. Find them, Magistrate. I'll help. Whatever you need."

"I need leads, but a smaller group is better for that." She looked at Joseph, a telepath with capabilities far superior to hers.

Petricia took his hand and spoke for both of them. "We'll come with you."

Rivka watched the overhead cranes and maintenance bots strip the spike-like transmitters off her ship and replace them with regularly spaced small devices that were little more than bumps.

Ankh, when will the ship be ready to go? she asked using her internal comm chip.

After their last mission, Ankh had grown more attentive about replying quickly and reasonably.

It'll be another eight hours. We cannot stop the process midway because then we'll lose the cloaking capability of the ship. This is the only upgrade for this visit.

She thanked Ankh before addressing her guests. "It'll be another eight hours before we can depart. There's plenty of time to get your stuff if you'd like."

"We travel light, but I guess we could grab a thing or two. I don't know if we'll need them or not."

"Eight hours. We'll depart as soon as the deck gang gives us clearance. Thank you for joining us on this one. I don't understand the mindset behind this kind of thing or those who fund it. None of it makes any sense to me."

"We will help you understand, Magistrate. Will we get guns?"

Rivka chuckled, then covered it. "Do you need them?"

"My question to you." Joseph turned it around.

"I don't think so. No guns to start with, but we have extras and some ridiculous firepower, too. A weapon that will defeat a mass assault on the ship."

"I should hope we would not need that, my lady," Joseph replied. "Come, dear."

Joseph and Petricia strolled away. She gripped his arm. His posture was stiff and military-like.

Not military. Aristocratic. He was from a different era where his wife was his queen and he the king. Rivka hadn't remembered him speaking so stiffly, but he didn't know her. Maybe retirement had returned him to his roots of classic language, of those who rescued damsels in distress. To a time when Joseph was finding his way.

Rivka returned to *Wyatt Earp* to chart their next moves, starting with going to the places where the warriors had been kidnapped. Both had been on short liberty, just a few days off.

A plan started to form for generating a lead since none were obvious. She needed to call Christina.

CHAPTER FOUR

Federation Base Station 11

Rivka stuffed the neutron pulse weapon into her pocket. She had asked Red and Lindy to go in wearing ballistic body armor and carrying railguns. There was no question regarding her authority when it came to Federation property like the space station.

Eight of them pounded through the corridors on their way to the station manager's office. Sahved walked beside Rivka while the SCAMPs Chaz and Dennicron walked behind them, with Joseph and Petricia in the back. The ever-vigilant bodyguards had the front and rear.

"I am the happiest anyone has ever been throughout existence at being allowed to rejoin your team. I am your humble servant."

"Sahved. We talked about superlatives. Good on Yemilore. Bad everywhere else. I am happy that you are pleased. We have a job to do, and you're an integral part of it. It's good to have you back.

"Where's your ballistic protection?" Rivka asked once she realized he wasn't wearing his chest protector.

He slapped his chest and looked around as if it had fallen off. His face dropped. "It appears that I have forgotten it. I am ashamed."

"Don't get yourself shot. Stay behind Red," Rivka replied. "And when we get back to the ship, get yourself enhanced, just in case you forget again. I don't want you to die, Sahved. We just got you back, and it would suck a whole lot to lose you again because I don't have the energy to train anyone else."

"That is most humbling. Thank you, I think."

"There's smoke coming off your back because of that burn, buddy!" Chaz called from behind.

Sahved twisted around to see if he was on fire.

Chaz tried to put on an innocent face, but his android body refused to cooperate, and his laugh subroutine kept overriding his command. He had a near-psychotic appearance as he transitioned rapidly back and forth between the looks. He hammered himself in the side of his head with the heel of his hand, which reset his facial expression motors.

"Guys," Rivka warned. "We're looking for people who are stealing our own to exploit their bodies. My apologies, Joseph and Petricia. We tend to keep things light no matter how horrible the situation. It's how we cope with the pain and misery."

"You should see TH in the thick of it," Joseph replied. "No offense taken, Magistrate."

They continued in silence to the central lift, which they

took to the very top of the station where the manager maintained his office.

When Rivka arrived, she found him waiting for them. "Such important visitors on a topic that is most distressing. I'm pleased to meet you, Magistrate, despite the situation surrounding your missing man." He held out his gloved hand. "I'm Nubeau Teak."

Rivka took his hand to shake and gripped his bare forearm with her other hand in a warm clasp. She saw his thoughts clearly. The alleged incident had been blown out of proportion. The warrior had skipped out. Teak was confident in the security of his station. Waste of his time.

"I assure you, Manager Teak, we are not wasting your time. Lance Reynolds needs to have confidence that his station managers will protect Federation personnel. I am already convinced that you are not taking this seriously. That is a problem."

Terror flashed through his mind.

Rivka almost felt bad about name-dropping, but her short tenure as a Magistrate had created a disdain for bureaucrats and then magnified it exponentially. Nubeau Teak was the perfect bureaucrat.

"Why isn't your office inside the station so you can rent this space out to maximize your profitability?" Rivka asked.

"I-I..." he stammered before falling silent. Then he weakly offered a defense. "Reynolds knew this was my office."

"No matter. I'll have the admin team conduct a full audit. But first, I want all the video from the time Private Elbinar was on the station. You'll transfer that material to my assistants Chaz and Dennicron. Better yet, give us access to your station's records."

"We don't have an AI yet. It's been difficult to find one."

Rivka smiled. "Not if you offer a good contract. I happen to know a number of sentient intelligences who might be interested. Give Chaz and Dennicron that, too. You see, the Embassy of the Singularity is in your personnel transport hangar bay right now. The ambassador would probably like to review how you treated your last SI and why they left. So much opportunity to improve!" she declared with a flourish and looked at her team.

The manager's face had turned pale and his shoulders slumped. "Of course," he agreed.

Dennicron stepped forward. "My name is Dennicron, and this is Chaz. We are representatives of the Singularity. If you'll simply log in to your system, we'll take care of the rest."

The station manager hesitated. The SIs had figured out that Dennicron worked best on men like Nubeau Teak. She smiled and flicked her hair back.

"Just a quick login. I won't be long."

"Okay." He tried to smile, but it was weak and fleeting. He accessed his terminal and held the chair for Dennicron to sit down. Her fingers flew across the access until she created a link directly to her mind. Within ten seconds, she had given herself and Chaz access to the core and every system run from it, which included the entirety of the station's databases. She planted a crawler to look for information related to Private Elbinar, along with a standard suite of audit tools that started analyzing the numbers the second she stood up.

"Thank you." She touched him gently on the hand and circled the desk to rejoin Chaz. Total time in the chair, sixteen seconds.

If he had done that with someone else, they could have destroyed the station from within. Dennicron was also looking for any viruses or tracker programs found in compromised systems.

"You're done?"

"I only needed one thing—to give myself access. We'll take care of that when we're back on the ship. You have my word that I will limit my activities to those authorized by the Magistrate. We will cause no damage to your system. Your station is safe with us."

Rivka glanced at Joseph, who watched Nubeau through unblinking eyes. She decided to energize the information collection.

"I believe the private was last seen in a bar. Can you tell us which one that was and who was on duty at the time?"

Nubeau slid into the recently vacated chair at his desk and pulled up the station's brief investigation. He started to sweat.

"I cannot."

"Because you don't know?" Rivka made it a statement. He shook his head.

"Dennicron?" Rivka looked at the SI, whose processors had run facial recognition through the station logs. She tallied the hits and checked the locations on the station blueprint.

"The ubiquitously named Supernova, Level Four, Section Fifty-One."

"How did you know that?" The station manager started to panic and looked from face to face.

"Because she's an investigator and takes her work seriously, unlike you and your team. We'll take it from here. Tell your people to cooperate. It's your only hope if you want to retain your position."

Any bravado or confidence he'd once had rapidly fled his shattered ego.

The team strolled back onto the elevator on their way to Level Four.

"I appreciate watching you work," Joseph said. "Do you always beat people up using the law like that?"

"I beat up people who deserve to be beat up. He didn't care about the missing warrior. He had done nothing about it. There's a name that fits. Weasel? Cheesedick? Pudknocker? I'm at a loss as to which is right."

"And you're usually so good with words," Red offered.

Sahved gave her his rapt attention. "Fascinating."

When they were in the privacy of the elevator, Rivka asked. "What did you see?"

Sahved replied, "I suspect the same things you saw. The title I would give him would be a self-serving bureaucrat. Nothing nefarious. It is all too common in governments and larger corporations. Bureaucrats have their place, Magistrate."

"I know, but not when they lord it over others. Being a bureaucrat doesn't make you better than the people you serve. I think that's lost all too often."

She chewed the inside of her cheek as she glowered at

the wall, trying to tamp down her almost unnatural hatred of all things quagmired within bureaucracies.

"Supernova, here we come. Can one of you people with a map in your head join me up front to lead the way?" Red asked, looking at Chaz and Dennicron.

Dennicron worked her way to the elevator doors to stand beside him.

"Fancy meeting you here," Red told her.

"We all came on the same ship. The Magistrate invited us along. I don't understand."

Lindy bumped him.

Red smiled over his shoulder. "It never stops being fun." He chuckled to himself.

"Ah. The dispensation of logic and reason to establish an alternate reality. You are a funny guy. I will kill you last," Dennicron replied.

"Hey! What?"

The doors opened, and Red had to tear his attention away from Dennicron to scan the area before stepping out. The SI walked unerringly with a purpose toward the Supernova bar, a place where warriors would congregate for cheap booze, bar food, and possible company.

"Any images of our missing man?" Rivka asked.

Chaz held up one finger, and after a brief pause, the Magistrate's datapad buzzed. She gave Chaz the thumbs-up, pulled out the device, and scrolled through the images.

She stopped at the one showing the private and a diminutive figure sitting at the bar. Rivka tapped it and scrolled forward until she found an image of them leaving the bar. "I want to find this woman. What race is she, Chaz?"

Rivka showed the image to the group. No one had seen the race before. Humanoid with trace elements of feline, giving her a lithe shape with fur instead of hair that grew in more places than just on her head.

"She's about as cute as a bug's ear," Red said after a glance.

Rivka knew she had him. "Do men like bug's ears?"

"Men are rather flexible in what they like. I won't expound, but if you wish to take a look…" He held out his arm while keeping his eyes ahead.

"No way," Rivka declined. Lindy blushed, but only for a moment. Soon enough, the lights dimmed in the section.

Joseph and Petricia could see well in the dark, as could the SCAMPs. Rivka's eyes were slightly oversized to help her, but Sahved was ill-equipped to deal with the change in illumination.

His question was straightforward. "Why is it dark here?"

"Because the darkness and a couple beers make the flexible zone pretty big. Those customers also tend to wave their credit chips like they're calling for a cab."

"I see," Sahved said while shaking his head. "No. I can't see at all. It is too dark down here. This is not normal."

"Dennicron?" Rivka asked.

"There are maintenance requests to fix the lighting. As soon as one is resolved, another crops up. It seems to be a perpetual thing. And more, Magistrate—the cameras in this area are out more than they are operational."

Rivka clenched her teeth. "I seem to have more questions for our station manager. As soon as we're done here,

I'll want to talk with the head of maintenance and then back to my favorite bureaucrat, Nubeau."

"You used to be one, if I'm not mistaken," Sahved remarked. "They are not all bad, are they, if you were one?"

"When I was one, a standard run-of-the-mill lawyer, I saw what we were doing as beneficial to the greater good. Administration ensured consistency in the application of the rules to give everyone a fair shake at whatever services were provided, whatever jurisprudence was applied, and whatever it took to establish a framework within which free people could thrive. But what I've seen since I became a Magistrate is that too many bureaucrats have lost sight of why they're doing what they do. It becomes a self-serving cesspool with the beneficiaries neck-deep in the shit." Rivka pointed to the well-lit bar sign up ahead.

Supernova.

"They can keep the bar lights on, it seems," Sahved noted, instantly changing into the observant investigator Rivka had hired.

She nodded at him but said it aloud to ensure he heard the message. "Those are the kinds of observations I need you to make. Well done, Sahved. Stay sharp, people. Let's be low profile."

Red shook his head without looking back and walked through the double-wide opening leading into the bar. It was open seating, with a humanoid bartender and a server of dubious ancestry leaning on the bar. There were four total customers in two pairs on the opposite side of the seating area.

Lindy stopped by the entrance, where she could look out. Red stood nearly back to back with her.

"Chaz." Red stopped the SI. "Can you watch into the dark beyond for us?"

"Of course. I see how that would help the team the most. Dennicron will handle the interrogation if needed."

Red tried not to roll his eyes. He caught Rivka's look. *Low key...*

Rivka headed for the bar, flanked by Dennicron and Sahved, while Joseph and Petricia meandered in behind them to take a spot at the far end of the bar.

The Magistrate flashed her creds. The bartender didn't bother looking.

"I'm Magistrate Rivka Anoa, and I'm here to investigate a missing person who was last seen in this bar."

The bartender shrugged. "I wasn't at work. That wasn't my shift. Can I get you something to drink? The bar is for paying customers only."

Rivka removed her datapad to show the picture of the private, the catlike alien, and the bartender beyond. It was the one talking to her.

"I'd appreciate not getting jacked around. This was seven days ago. I need you to dig deep and tell me what you know." As he leaned forward, she gripped his arm. "Please."

He'd thought the woman was a hooker playing the lonely military man's heartstrings like a virtuoso. He hadn't seen her before but expected to see her again. Rivka let go before his thoughts strayed too far into the erotic.

"Do you know what race that woman is?"

The bartender shrugged again. "Like I said, it wasn't me. Now, if you'll excuse me, I have customers."

Joseph winked at Rivka.

Sahved frowned. "He is lying." The Yemilorian turned to the server, who had been trying to inch away but was stopped by Dennicron. "What about you? What do you know about the Federation's missing man?"

She was more accommodating. "He was here but left of his own accord with the woman of his dreams who he met in a bar. It's the age-old story of love and betrayal."

"May I ask, what betrayal?" Sahved pressed.

"To those he owed. He was military, right? He found his woman and didn't want to leave her. Is that so far-fetched?"

Sahved didn't have the experience to make that call. Dennicron jumped into the conversation. "That is one of many possibilities that we're looking into. Would you know where they went from here?"

"There are pay-by-the-hour rooms not far from here. Two side corridors down. Many couples, and I use the term loosely, go there from here and then return as singles once the money is paid."

Sahved nodded knowingly, which made Rivka wonder what he knew about the world of prostitution. It wasn't illegal, but many of the activities surrounding it were.

Like theft and kidnapping.

"I appreciate your information," Rivka said, holding out her hand. The server took it, and they shook. No subterfuge ran through her bored mind. She wondered when her shift would be over, disappointed that the distraction had only taken three minutes.

Rivka was ready to go. She had gotten the answers she needed to keep moving forward.

Joseph and Petricia saluted with their shot glasses of

whiskey before downing them and ordering a second round from the bartender. Rivka leaned against the bar, killing time while Joseph pursued his look into the bartender's mind. She watched the patrons, who kept their heads bowed.

"Might as well ask if they were here," Rivka said and sauntered to the first couple, helping herself to a seat at their table. She slid her datapad across the table. "Have you seen either of these two people?"

They both shook their heads. Rivka stood and walked around to their side of the table, where she put the pad down again. "Are you sure?" She brushed their arms. No.

The woman was a prostitute working the guy for at least a meal. He was trying to leave without paying.

"You better pay your bill," Rivka told him. She snatched her datapad away and headed for the other table. The two there immediately stood, but Red pointed at them to sit back down.

"Stop hassling my patrons," the bartender said without enthusiasm. It was for public consumption, to endear himself to the paying customers. Protector and savior.

He was neither of those things, but he wouldn't tell Rivka anything that happened in the bar. The patrons saw that, too.

Rivka waved at him and continued to the table, where she showed the images and touched them both. A nice couple on vacation from their home planet in the Virant Trinary. "Whatever brought you here?"

"Good food?" the male replied.

"Food?" Rivka looked at Sahved, and he instantly

caught on. He headed for the back to see where the meals were prepared, and more importantly, who was doing it.

He went through a nondescript door into an area behind the bar and was gone for no more than five seconds. He shook his head. "Chef-bot 3000," he stated.

"Thank you all for your time," Rivka told those in the bar. Joseph and Petricia threw back their final shots and stood on steady feet. They were enhanced and mostly immune to the effects of normal alcohol.

Lindy and Chaz took point since they'd heard what the server had said. The rent-a-room place.

What did you find out? Rivka asked, using her internal comm chip.

He has a vested interest in the trade since he is a part-owner in the rooms for rent, Joseph replied.

Well done. I only saw that he figured her for a hooker, not that he wanted her to rent an overpriced room from him. Good information. Dennicron, can you find if the private paid for a room and if he did, which one?

Yes, I have all the information. He did not rent a room, but there were two rentals during the timeframe where the woman was in the bar. One was a couple that appears legitimate. The other was made by someone named Spiriva from a planet called Cobilor.

Rivka reached for her datapad but stopped. "Tell me what you know about Cobilor."

A K-class warm planet that was a former Yollin colony that converted to the Etheric Federation upon the overthrow of the Empire. Cobilor is on the far side of the galaxy. Its people have a distinct blue tint while being tall with multiple appendages.

Rivka smiled. *Next, you'll tell me that no one from Cobilor has been on this station in quite some time, if ever.*

Exactly, Magistrate. Spiriva is probably a fake name and profile. I have turned it over to the Singularity to find all there is to find about the one who created this persona, and we shall digitally track them on board this station.

Rivka bobbed her head as she contemplated. Fake names might have been created out of thin air, but once people created a digital profile, they left a trail. Ankh and the ambassador had taught her that.

More good news, and out of all of it, this tidbit would get her closer to the private. She was convinced that he had been kidnapped, not willingly abandoned his role with the Bad Company. Those people were fanatically loyal, as Christina had confirmed in their short but fruitful phone call.

"Where's the rental office?" Rivka asked. Chaz stopped and pointed back the way they'd come. "Don't tell me it's not co-located with the rooms."

Chaz kept his mouth shut. Dennicron answered. "It's not co-located with the rooms."

"Let's split up. Chaz, Lindy, Joseph, and Petricia, check out the room rental spaces. I'll go to the rental office and see what we can learn when it comes to our mysterious Mister Spiriva, who is not who he claimed to be, and this woman, who is also not who she appeared to be."

CHAPTER FIVE

Federation Base Station 11

The office was small and smelled of cigarettes even though smoking was frowned upon throughout the Federation. There was a walk-up window, but Rivka bypassed that and followed Red inside. He loomed over the grubby old woman behind a desk who was watching a pornographic video, probably blasting it because she was hard of hearing.

The Magistrate showed her creds and introduced herself. "I want everything you have regarding an individual who rented a room from you. Name was Spiriva."

She gave Rivka the finger, which made the Magistrate wonder if she could see.

I already have the information from their files, Magistrate, Dennicron noted.

"What kind of racket are you running?" Rivka grabbed the woman's upraised digit and twisted just enough to get her attention but not enough to cause pain to dominate her thoughts.

"Who are you?" she demanded. Rivka maintained her grip.

"I'm the Magistrate, and I'm investigating a crime that took place in your rooms."

"Only crime out there is someone keeps popping the lights and cameras."

Rivka closed her eyes and tilted her head back. "That's the only crime we see, which is why it's committed. What is going on in your rooms, mainly theft and kidnapping?"

"Ain't no theft or kidnapping. At least, I'm not getting a cut. Pustule-sucking lowlife titwads." The old woman tried to jerk her hand free. Rivka let her go after seeing in her mind that she was put out by not getting a cut of the activities in the rooms. She pulled a cigarette from the drawer, lit it, and blew the smoke at Rivka. Red leveled his railgun.

Rivka gave him the look of wonder that said, "I wonder what the hell you're doing."

"I can shoot it out of her mouth."

The woman took an obscenely long drag, then pulled the cigarette out of her mouth and ran her tongue around her lips before blowing the smoke at Vered. His stomach heaved, and he gagged. He looked forlornly at the Magistrate. She sympathized with her bodyguard.

"I'm going to check the room he rented." She turned to Dennicron.

"Room Four tac Forty-Seven tac One Fifteen Bravo."

"I need access, so please key me to it."

"Gotta pay before you get access." The woman stood. She had Rivka by a solid fifty kilos, but none of it was muscle.

"Lady," Red interrupted, "give the Magistrate access."

She guided the cigarette toward her mouth. Red slapped it out of her hand before she could take a drag.

"Smoking is nasty. Now would be a good time to quit."

She snarled. "I like it, and I paid good money for that. You owe me one doobie!"

"Dennicron, can you confirm our access?"

"Done," she replied immediately. "All rooms."

Rivka twirled her finger in the air. Time to go.

"Lady," Red said after the others had filed out, "you need to rethink your life decisions."

"My life is over. Smoking and eating junk is the fastest of the slow deaths. Maybe you could just shoot me now and take care of it? No one would miss old Bertha."

"You're probably right about that, but I'm not going to help you. Go find some other lackey. It wouldn't take hardly anything to turn this into a decent establishment. Going out ugly is your choice. Going out as a decent person is your choice, too." He left before she could reply.

Rivka slightly inclined her head. "I'm impressed, Vered. You're telling people to change their lives and not looking to pound them first."

"I didn't want to get any nasty on me," he replied. "Nothing more. None of you pukecicles should think I've grown soft because I haven't. I'll kick your ass upside down and backwards if you start spreading your vile rumors."

"Red is turning into a nice guy and other vile rumors. Stay tuned for more," Rivka quipped.

Sahved looked confused, tilting his head back and forth as he studied Red's face. "I am the poorest investigator ever. I don't know what's going on. Who is doing what to whom and where? Is Red nice or not? Is this a change from before? I have so many questions."

"There you have it, Sahved. You have concisely summed up our entire understanding of Red."

"I don't have any conclusions. Only questions."

"Exactly. Red at his finest."

"Finest what? Niceness?" Sahved remained confused as Rivka focused on the way ahead.

"Thanks, Dennicron. It's nice having complete access to the station. You were masterful, working with the station manager."

"Thank you!" The SI almost instantly beamed at the praise. The expression subroutines were running like they were supposed to. The SIs were getting better by the day, unlike toddlers, who take years. Within weeks, she expected the two would be indistinguishable from humans. Well, except for visual anomalies around joints and other moving parts where the construction material didn't flex as well as skin, like the fingers, elbows, knees, and feet.

You should be able to access the rooms, but wait until we get there, Rivka passed to the rest of the team.

Rivka waved as she passed Supernova for the second time in five minutes. Sahved mirrored her motion before leaning close. "Why are we waving?" he whispered.

"Just to let them know we still love them," Rivka replied.

"We do?"

"Absolutely," Red said, holding his thumb up over his shoulder where Sahved could see it.

"I will study this later. I have much to learn."

"That is true," Rivka admitted.

"Does that mean something you told me earlier was untrue?"

"Everything I say is a lie," she told him.

While he was twisting about with that, they met the others in the darkened hallway that held the rooms for rent. A sign over the entrance read, *Rest your weary head, travelers, for you have come far.* Someone had added in heavy black marker, *Your boner deserves attention. Right here. Right now.*

Red started to laugh and couldn't stop. "This guy is a genius."

Lindy shook her head.

Rivka stared down the hallway at the single light that worked at the far end. She strolled down, leaning close to read the plates above each access panel. When she reached the room that had been rented by Spiriva, she waved her hand over the panel, and the door slid open. Rivka stepped in to block the door and keep it open.

"Has anyone else rented this room since Spiriva?"

"Two rentals occurred for one hour each," Dennicron answered.

"With a good fifty-five minutes going to waste. I think we'll still find something. Scan it, you two. You have the systems to make short work of any crime scene investigation."

She leaned on the doorframe and watched as the SCAMPs strolled around the room, checking the floor and the other surfaces while ignoring the well-used bed. The bathroom had been cleaned but not well.

Chaz and Dennicron consulted each other while staring at the carpet in the center of the room. Dennicron testing it by running a heel over the area. Chaz deferred.

"We believe that the private fell right here and was carried away by persons unknown."

Rivka hurried into the room and leaned down, trying to see what the SIs had noted. "You got all of that from this?"

"Yes. Our full report will be added to your case file. The depth of carpet compression is visible because this carpet is old with a weakened support pad. There are a number of fibers that are upright to outline the main impact, and only five people have walked through this area since."

"Amazing. Thank you for that. It's like having my own lab with me at all times."

Chaz and Dennicron nodded at each other.

"Anything on the temptress?"

"Yes. There are hairs, looking like cat hairs, embedded within the indent. I would guess that she was beneath him when he fell." Chaz secured samples in a small baggie and shook it before the others as if it were a great prize.

Rivka frowned. "That might suggest he wasn't the only victim. Both of them? Is this blood trade-related? I need to contact Grainger and get more on why he thinks this was blood trade." She looked at Joseph and Petricia, who were hovering in the corridor. "I'm sorry. I hope I haven't wasted your time."

"There's only so much golf one can play, young lady." Joseph bowed with a sweep of his hand.

Rivka didn't ask if that meant time invested investigating the case was wasted.

"Next stop, Maintenance," Rivka declared. *And in the*

meantime, Clevarious, get me Grainger. See if I can walk and talk at the same time.

They secured the room on their way out.

Rivka! It's now morning. I'm sipping my steaming-hot java, watching comedy vids in my underwear, and wondering how my favorite Magistrate's case is going.

That's what you do in the morning?

No. I'm jacking you because you woke me up last night. I think it was last night. I can never remember. What did I say?

It's what you didn't say. We have an unidentified race where a cat vixen drew the warrior away from the bar. But we are in possession of information that suggests she may also have been a victim of the kidnapping. And yes, I am convinced it was a kidnapping. The private didn't bail on the Bad Company, Rivka explained.

This is just for your ears, Rivka. Lance discovered a few of the wealthy ambassadors were starting to look younger when there was no reason for it. Through methods available to him, he was able to surreptitiously check a blood sample.

Rivka stopped walking, bringing the group to a grinding halt. They stood around trying to look inconspicuous while she stared with a blank expression, looking little more than a drug-addled zombie.

And if there was any note of that in official paperwork, it could bring down the Federation through an open rebellion because one shouldn't be conducting covert testing on the trusted members of the council. I understand. What planets, so we can dig deep into the finances and find where the payments are going?

Delegor, Mastus, and Foromme Three. Rivka didn't know

anything about the planets except that they weren't in this sector of space. They had a big Gate jump ahead of them.

We won't leave a trace of this investigation unless we find them via a different route. We don't punish users, but suppliers deserve our full ire. The ambassadors will not be involved, but all of a sudden, they may no longer be able to juice with the blood of victims.

As it should be. Find the architects and bring it down. Nothing public on this. It's all done out of the limelight.

You know me, Grainger. I never upset the apple cart.

I don't think you understand the definition of the word "never." Go get 'em, Magistrate. Grainger signed off.

Rivka blinked and found herself standing in the middle of an open area with her seven teammates standing around her, trying to look inconspicuous.

"New leads," she told them. "I need to butter the Singularity's muffin because I have a task for which they are uniquely suited in order to attack this thing from the buyer's perspective."

"The buyers…" Ice hung from Joseph's words. His eyebrows furrowed in a look that allowed no ambiguity. Joseph held the buyers as culpable as their suppliers.

"Are you going to go werewolf on them and rip them limb from limb?"

"Vampire. Well, we used to be, but not anymore. No, good Magistrate, we shall not rend flesh except in our own defense, but I *will* use my unique talents to insert into a user's mind an overwhelming fear of needles to the point of apoplexy. Even contemplating getting poked will cause them debilitating pain. I think it apropos. And no, I'm not a Magistrate. I don't have the authority to punish the guilty, but I will do it because of what the blood trade does to its victims."

Rivka nodded slightly while looking at the deck. "It's not illegal to be an addict."

"Punishment is coming for all involved," Joseph replied in a low voice. He stared Rivka down.

She wouldn't budge. "Let me address them first, please. If they are in my care, I'll need you to leave them alone."

"I can't guarantee that, but I shall afford you the respect you deserve."

Rivka wasn't sure that meant she could trust Joseph and Petricia not to go rogue. He was one of Terry Henry's closest friends, which earned him as much latitude as she could give. She could ask for no more. "Fair enough. I appreciate your insight thus far. We'll find them, Joseph, Petricia. And we will take them down."

"That's a promise I can get behind and why we're here. This trade cannot be allowed to continue. Every tendril. Every associate. Every medical professional. And most importantly, the kidnapping team. Everyone involved. Only then will we return to Keeg Station and resume our daily golf."

"We have a golf simulator onboard *Wyatt Earp,*" Red offered, using the opportunity to distract Joseph so they could get on with the investigation.

"Only then will we resume our daily golf," Joseph reiterated.

"One can only play so much during retirement," Rivka added, paraphrasing Joseph's earlier words. "Let's get back to the witnesses. Maintenance awaits."

CHAPTER SIX

Federation Base Station 11, Maintenance Office

"This big station, and there's only one person who works here?" Rivka blurted. The small office was filled with computer servers, paper files, a receiving station, and a single workstation behind the high table where customers could register their complaints. The office was a dingy tan, and oddly, only half the overhead lights were functional.

"Shows you how much they care." The frazzled middle-aged woman pointed at the ceiling. "I'm given an army of bots, though, but no AI to program them. I have a bunch of specific programs I can drop in: change a lightbulb, fix an electrical circuit, clear a blockage in water reclamation, maybe a hundred more. Most of the maintenance needs are minimal."

"What about the corridor around Section Four tac Forty-Seven?" Rivka asked.

The maintenance chief, one Garner Rose Hoskin, pulled up the location on the computer. "The only maintenance issues in that area are the broken cameras and lights. Every time I have something fixed, someone vandalizes it. I stopped fixing things, and they stopped getting broken. I know that's not the cause and effect we're going for, but there's only so much that I can do."

"No one complains about the lights and cameras?" Rivka sat on the edge of the desk and watched her face. The Magistrate didn't need to touch her to know she was telling the truth.

"No one that matters." The woman ran a hand through her tousled and wild hair. "If they cared, we'd have an AI running this station."

"They are called 'SIs' now, for 'sentient intelligence,' which is a different issue. Let me introduce you to a couple who work with me. Chaz and Dennicron."

The two stepped forward and nodded.

"No shit! That's amazing." She jumped to her feet. "You guys look amazing." She worked her way close and studied their faces and said for a third time, "Amazing!"

"Excuse me!" Chaz stopped the woman's hand as she reached out to touch him. "You're going in the right direction if you want your ass slapped."

She started to laugh but threw her hands up in surrender. "I've not personally met one of your kind before. Do you *all* have bodies? I thought you lived within computer systems."

"We do, but we now have mobility platforms, too, so we aren't tied to the system and, in essence, slaves. Sentient creatures should not own other sentient creatures. Freedom is intoxicating."

Rose crossed her arms and leaned against her desk. She glanced at Rivka. "Do you know any SIs looking for work?"

"So happens, we know *all* the SIs." Rivka smiled. "The Embassy of the Singularity is parked in the station's hangar bay."

"What will it take to bring one into the fold?"

Chaz stepped forward. "A good contract, but that's not what we're here for. We're investigating a kidnapping. It happened in the corridor where the cameras are nonfunctional. We'll need a complete track of the broken cameras that lead from Section One Forty-Seven to a place where an object the size of a person can be put on board a ship."

They already had the information but wanted to see how Rose addressed their concerns.

She brought up the map and built a route from the rental room to the main hangar bay. "I never noticed that. Looks like this has been in the works for a while. My God. I've been complicit in people trafficking." She stumbled around her desk and flopped into her seat. "What have I done?"

"You've done nothing wrong," Rivka told her. "You are given no resources to keep a station this size functional. Cameras and lights are a security issue. Why isn't Federation Security all over this?"

"We don't have Federation Security. It's been sub-contracted to a private firm. We're on the third company in eighteen months."

"Each one cheaper than the last, I suspect."

"The last one pulled chocks and bailed three days ago. We're running with minimal security right now as a new contractor ramps up, so I expect the criminal elements might get more bold."

"More bold than kidnapping a Bad Company warrior?" Rivka looked at Chaz and Dennicron. "Chaz, I want you to stay here and give Rose a hand with her maintenance duties. We're going back to talk with the soon-to-be-former station manager. And then put out a contract for an SI to take over station duties. We need someone on board as soon as possible. We can't have what we have going on here, independent of kidnapping. I will not have it!"

"Of course, Magistrate." Chaz sidled around the desk and crouched next to Rose. Because of Dennicron, he had full access to the station's systems. "Let's start knocking down these work orders, shall we?"

They left Rose after she delivered a short but effusive outpouring of gratitude.

Rivka and the remaining six took the elevator straight to the top level, where they found three people working in the office while the station manager sat on a secretary's desk, chatting with her. When he saw the Magistrate, he rocketed to his feet, nearly dumping the poor woman out of her chair. With a rushed apology, he hurried to meet Rivka.

"How can I help you?" he tripped over himself to say. "Any suspects in custody?"

She stared at him until he withered.

"May I use your comm terminal, please?"

"Of course, of course!" He led the way to his desk and logged in, then slid out of the way.

Rivka considered who best to call and decided to go right to the top. She tapped keys to link through her ship to let Clevarious handle the connection details. "Lance Reynolds, please."

The manager started drumming his fingers compulsively while his foot tapped the floor of the top-level executive suite.

"Kor'ban, so nice to talk with you. I expect the General is not available. I need to talk with him, but I can keep it under two minutes."

The voice from the other end replied, "Then I'll transfer you in. He'll be glad of the interruption, Magistrate Anoa. He never feels like you are wasting his time, but there's still the issue of the cat."

"Sorry about that. Humans have never successfully owned cats. It's the other way around, I believe. I was powerless on that issue."

"I see. Transferring you in."

Red chuckled, turning away to keep from looking like he was laughing at the station manager.

Damn cats.

"General. Magistrate Rivka Anoa. Quick brief. You know my mission. I started on Station Eleven to explore where the private disappeared. Much of the data I need isn't available because criminals have taken hold and can use this as a refuge from authority. I'd like to replace the station manager with someone competent, specifically an SI. I'll work with the Singularity to find a suitable replacement. And I am making progress on the issue of your concern."

"Make it happen, Rivka. Send status reports to me when you can. Is the station manager with you?"

"I'm using his terminal. Here."

Rivka smiled at the ghostly-pale Nubeau Teak.

"Lance Reynolds wishes to speak to you."

She let him have the spot in front of the screen. "I'm taking steps, General! I'll fix it, I swear."

"You're fired. I expect the Magistrate has already locked you out of your access. Get on the next flight that'll take you anywhere off that station. Reynolds out."

Dennicron tipped her chin toward the Magistrate. It was done.

"Your inevitable demise came quickly and will hopefully result in a rapid turnaround of this station as a safe refuge for travelers Federation-wide. Any time you let crime take root where they can kidnap a serving member of the military with impunity because your fucking security contractor is in on it is the last time you'll be in charge of any fucking thing!" By the time Rivka ended, she found herself shouting into his face. She smoothed her jacket. "Get your trash and get out. Dennicron, next flight?"

"Mister Teak has a seat on the flight that leaves in one hour for the interior planets before ending at Yoll."

"Good. Get on that flight, please. You can leave now." Rivka had lost patience with him after his first two sentences earlier that day. Now she was done with him.

Red took him by the arm to guide him toward the elevator. The bodyguard punched the button and shoved him in once it arrived. He watched him without comment or gesture until the doors closed.

"Good. Let's see what the ambassador has to say." Rivka switched to her internal comm chip. *Ambassador Erasmus, we have a unique opportunity for an SI to be the station manager of Federation Border Station Eleven. Can you make any recommendations?*

I am pleased with this opportunity. Thank you, Magistrate. I would like one of our newest SCAMP-enabled citizens to assume the position, but I think the soonest one can get here is three days unless we go get her. Say, in Destiny's Vengeance *and then meet back up with you? I get the impression you'll be following a lead elsewhere.*

You are properly impressed, Rivka replied. *As long as you are comfortable with the person who will fill the position, the Federation is comfortable. Thank you for your help. By the way, I have a job I need from your people.*

Dennicron has already passed your needs to us. We are working on it, but it is a big job, dissecting payments from major corporations in relatively minor sums to an unknown entity hiding behind a shell corporation. None of them will use their personal funds to make these payments, Magistrate. We've asked Lauton for a hand. And thank you for referring to us as people.

"Excellent," Rivka said aloud. *Of course. What else would you be? Don't answer that. I'm sure there are terms I don't want to hear. Welcome to management. Tell your person not to be a dick.*

Erasmus was confused. *She can't. Chrysanthemum selected the female form for her SCAMP.*

I assure you, she can. I'll be back to check on her, hopefully soon. When are you leaving?

We will return in two hours, well before the work is done on Wyatt Earp, Erasmus replied. The small office staff milled about, trying to look like they were doing their jobs while being unsure of what had happened.

We have some more digging to do. Someone *saw which ship*

took a body-sized crate out of here. It happened in a small window. Good luck.

I don't think we require luck, but we shall embrace your kind regards and say, same to you.

Rivka blinked since she'd been staring while talking with Erasmus, then spoke to the office workers. "Yes, that just happened. Your old boss is gone. The new boss is called Chrysanthemum. She's a sentient intelligence but is contained within an android body, not unlike Dennicron."

"That woman is a robot?" the youngest of the admin staff asked.

"No. That woman is a woman who happens to be a living creature within a manufactured body, driving it around like a paraplegic would a wheelchair or a hover-chair. A vehicle to support a fabulous mind. Chrysanthemum will need help, a lot of help because she will have little experience in directing a workforce, but she will learn quickly. I expect the station will start running like we need it to within days. Do any of you know what's up with the security contractor? I have seen no security uniforms on the station."

"There aren't many, and they keep to themselves."

"Does that apply to the new company, too?"

"New company?"

"Started three days ago or somewhere thereabout."

"No idea," the secretary replied.

Our boy Nubeau didn't hire them for their brains, Red suggested. Rivka scowled at him but only for a moment.

"Where are the security offices?" Rivka asked.

"Level Nine. There are signs once you get off the elevator," the oldest of the three young women replied.

Rivka motioned toward Red, who mashed the call button. "Keep doing what you're doing. Your new boss will be here shortly and soon thereafter, I expect your work will be significantly streamlined. You'll only do those things that add value to the entire station. Good luck," she told them.

Sometimes people needed luck. She wanted to think their lives would be better, but maybe they liked working for Teak with no performance expectations. Rivka violently disagreed. People should have more self-respect than that. She looked from face to face before getting on the elevator, but she didn't get the feeling they were happy with the change.

"Wait," she said and stepped off. She held out her hand. "I thank you for your patience during this trying time."

The first administrative assistant was worried about her job, as was the second. The third knew she couldn't compete if her good looks were removed from the equation. She was worried about losing her job, too.

"None of you need to worry about your jobs. Help the new station manager assimilate. Teach her and learn from her. I'll make a note that she's not to make any personnel changes for at least two weeks. You have plenty of time to show her your value, all of you. Be the team that gets it done. Be the team that runs a station people are proud to call home. And if you have any influence, there's a woman on the fourth level who runs the rooms for rent. Get her to stop smoking and maybe eat healthy, walk for fitness. Bring her back to the world of the living."

The youngest made a face. "People still do that?"

"It's not illegal," Rivka answered. "But there are cheaper

ways to occupy your time. Show her she has something to live for."

Rivka walked into the elevator, and the door closed before she turned around.

Sahved tapped her on the shoulder. "Was he that bad? On Yemilore, he would have been average as far as managers. Not good. Not bad. Just average."

"Remind me not to go back to Yemilore."

"Magistrate?" Sahved asked.

She looked up at him to continue.

"Don't go to Yemilore."

Rivka stared at Sahved, but he didn't look away. His eyes were different, making him capable of winning every staring contest.

Joseph cleared his throat. Rivka turned to him. "You did a good thing there. Those young ladies are like Yemilorian managers, neither good nor bad. Nothing but untapped potential. They are all better than they believe."

Petricia raised her hand. Rivka smiled at the naïveté of the gesture.

"I find this fascinating. So many disparate threads that lead us inexorably forward. If we dismantle the infrastructure as we go, then we will drive them before us like stampeding cattle." Petricia used the Earth reference, having spent much more time there than in space with the beef-alternative bistok.

"Exactly that. The Magistrate is coming. And their fear will grow, which will magnify the risk to our person. Are the lines running?" Rivka wondered.

"The second we stepped aboard the station, Magistrate," Red replied. "You were good on the swearing until you got going with the station manager. That line is closed while all others are still open. And new twist this time, they continue to take bets on unclosed lines."

"No running. No blood," Rivka stated. Those were the two main lines Federation officials far and wide bet on in a pool that had grown massive. Colorful language, first punch, first arrest, and case closed. The remainder continued to build value for the winner who bet on the exact time of an event. To date, they had never had a "no blood" and "no running" case. Most times, both lines closed.

Only Rivka was allowed to bet the last line and she always did, knowing that one day, she'd walk away from a case without getting chased or shot at or one of her team injured.

She didn't expect that on this case. Next stop, she'd be wearing ballistic protection too, just like anyone else who went into the lion's den. The rough side of the case was coming. She could feel it in her bones.

CHAPTER SEVEN

Federation Base Station 11, Security Office

"This looks a little better than the maintenance office," Red said before stepping forward. The double doors separated in the middle and slid to the sides. Inside looked bright and clean. Two humanoids in security uniforms leaned on their desks.

Rivka flashed her creds. "I'm Magistrate Rivka Anoa, and I'd like to talk with whoever is in charge."

"Ain't here, lady," one of the two said in a gruff voice. The alien's skin appeared to be smooth like that of a lizard, with similar forest-colored mottling.

"I figured that. Where can I find this absent head of security?"

She tried to work her way around the receiving counter, but the half-door was secured. Neither guard moved to open it. Rivka nodded at Lindy. In two steps, one guard vaulted the counter, rotating past her hand braced on top and slipping to the other side.

"Hey!" the second guard said, finally rising from his chair.

Lindy backed toward the door, keeping the two in view. Once there, she flipped the latch.

"He ain't here because he's on his way. We just got this contract, and it so happens that this quality talent was readily available." He joined his fellow in standing and smoothed the front of the uniform.

"How long have you been on the job?"

"Since six this morning. We're on until six when the night shift comes in."

"How many days," Rivka clarified.

"Since six this morning," the guard reiterated.

"How were you available? Were you already on the station?"

"No, lady. We came in on a freighter hoping to find mining jobs, but this popped up, and here we are." They looked at each other and nodded vigorously.

"Was there any training? Do you have any certifications?" At this point, Rivka realized these two and the security company that had won the contract after the others walked was Chrysanthemum's problem.

"What passed-down notes do you have from the previous contractor? Any unsolved cases, perps in lock up, stuff like that?"

"Nah. Nothing handed down. It was like we had a clean slate. So here we are, keeping the station secure so you can go about your business with confidence and peace of mind."

"That sounds right," Red mumbled.

The guard pointed at a sign over the door with the words he had just repeated.

"What are you doing to make those words come true?"

"What's with the interrogation? We're the ones who ask the questions around here. What are you doing to keep the peace because you're interfering with mine, and that should be a crime? Maybe you're the one should be locked up!"

Red didn't take his eyes off them. "Can people be this stupid?" he asked loud enough for them to hear.

"There are no answers for us here. Joseph?"

"Definitely no answers," Joseph confirmed.

Rivka turned back to the two guards while Lindy joined them in front of the counter. "Your new boss's boss will be here in a couple hours. I hope you'll be able to tell her that you've done something besides stonewall a Federation Magistrate."

"Magistrate? I thought you said 'matches gate,' and that don't mean nothing to me. Magistrate. Yeah. We heard of them. Aren't you a little short to be one?"

Red whispered, "You know you want to hit them, just enough to toss them over their desks and give them a little nap."

"Good luck, gentlemen," Rivka told them before walking out. Both men screamed in pain and held their heads. Joseph covered his smile with his hand and coughed, followed by clearing his throat.

Clodagh, spin up Wyatt Earp. *We'll be heading to the other side of the galaxy. First stop is Delegor.*

"You have access to the security systems, don't you?" Rivka asked after they left the office.

"Yes, of course. We have access to everything."

She shook her head slowly. "Thank goodness. I didn't want to go back in there."

"Not up for kicking their asses, or are you just trying to stymy the betting line?" Red asked.

"They shouldn't be in their positions. They have no idea what they're doing. It's probably best they don't get involved with any criminals on the station since they'd be the ones most likely to get hurt. Can't hold stupid against people, but I can hold it against those who hired them into that position. And I'll need all the information on the previous company. Chaz, start the search. Find where they came from and where they went. Sahved, I'll need your skills on Delegor as I can't be seen investigating an ambassador. You, Joseph, and Petricia will be running down leads."

Joseph rubbed his hands together and smiled.

The team walked into the hangar bay. Sahved held up one of his three fingers. "I believe the work crew that was on when the private was carried out may be available now." He brought out his datapad to show an image of the crew in the background when four shrouded figures guided a hovergurney through the air and onto a waiting transport.

"Find me that transport, too. How was this image available? I thought all the cameras had been rendered inoperable?"

"All the official cameras were not working, but this is a sequence from a private firm's feed. They were watching their own ship."

"How did you get this? You've been with me the whole time." Rivka glanced at Chaz, who was making eyes at Sahved. "Good job," she told both of them.

She took a closer look at the images. "She's walking with the others. She doesn't look like their captive. Distinctively larger. I feel that we have three males and a female they use for the honeytrap. We're looking for four individuals. Gait appears comparable. Are they all cat people? Where are they from?"

"They are Furlorians," Dennicron replied definitively. "A refugee race that recently entered the Federation sphere from Krawlas after their planet was invaded by the warlike Wyyvan. Most of them have returned to Krawlas to reestablish their race, following their Federation-supported victory over their enemy."

"I guess they have some entrepreneurs in their midst." Rivka chewed on the name. "Furry, with tails. Catlike. We can deal with them. They shouldn't be hard to track. Thanks, D. Sahved, they're your lead. Joseph and Petricia, if you'd go with him, I'd appreciate it."

"As you wish, my lady," Joseph bowed. Petricia waved, and the three strolled toward the on-shift deck gang.

Rivka watched them go. She only had to say one word. "Red." He nodded and followed them. The others followed the Magistrate to their ship, dodging heavy equipment to get to the hatch.

As soon as she was aboard, she started giving orders. "Clevarious, tell me when the *Vengeance* returns. Clodagh! Damn. I forget..." She looked at the cockpit hatch like the answer was there. It wasn't. Rivka couldn't see anyone inside the cockpit, so she continued toward her quarters, stopping just before she went in.

She smiled at the revelation of memory and hurried back to find her chief engineer and de facto captain. Tiny Man Titan's yapping gave her away. In the cockpit, Rivka found her lying on the deck. Clodagh smiled and waved. Titan blocked Rivka from getting too close to his human.

"You furious little beast! You better protect the baby with equal aplomb." Rivka's hand darted out to catch him under the chin and scratch before he could snap at her. His little tail started wagging. "I wanted to know how you're feeling, but this can't be good."

"My back was hurting. The cool metal feels good."

"Is Cole giving you back and foot rubs?" Rivka stood and crossed her arms.

"Not as much as I'd like."

"Do you need me to give him an attitude adjustment, as Red would say?"

"I better not. I need to convince him it's the right thing to do." Clodagh rolled to her side and struggled to sit up. Rivka dove past Titan to help her. Once she was on her feet, she looked aft. "I need to check the coolant pumps. We've been running hard. Despite all the good Ankh does, he doesn't get his hands dirty with the big mechanical stuff."

"I thought he built robots to do the dirty work?"

"That's one way to look at it. They aren't as good as me. You can't beat a good pair of Mark One eyeballs, if you'll excuse me. Did I hear that we're getting underway soon?"

"As soon as the upgrades to the hull are finished."

"The system will need to be calibrated after that. I hesitate to ask, but how much time can you give us?"

"If Ankh lets us use *Destiny's Vengeance* when we get to Delegor, then we'll have a day, maybe two before we head to Mastus and finally to Foromme Three."

Clodagh stared at the wall as she contemplated their route. "Those are a long way out there."

"I had heard of them but had no idea where they were. That will be the farthest out I've been. It's like we work among the stars or something. The beauty of space. Maybe there's a nebula in the area or a ringed planet to see."

"I better get to work. I can't have the boss mad at me."

Rivka laughed. "There's no chance of that. Do what you have to do, and I'll ask Red to help Cole understand his role in the relationship."

"Red? What would he know?"

Rivka held up her ring finger and drew a circle around it with her pointer. "Whatever Lindy wants. Don't let Red fool you. He knows how good he's got it. Cole should feel the same way."

"Maybe we'll get a cat," Clodagh taunted.

"Where did that come from? Clevarious! Save me. If anyone tries to bring a cat onboard, please sound the alarm and seal all hatches. We'll send them out the airlock once we reach orbit."

"She's kidding, C. No one is going out the airlock." Clodagh touched the Magistrate's shoulder on her way out. Titan barked once more before running after her.

Rivka climbed into the captain's chair. "Lock us in, Clevarious, and bring up the case files. Consolidate what you have on the ambassador from Delegor and put it on the main screen.

"Wouldn't it be better in your hologrid?"

"Probably, but I'm here and comfortable. Remember when this was the only refuge?"

"I think that was *Peacekeeper* and Chaz. He told me about it. A tiny ship, not befitting one of your stature."

Rivka looked away from the screen, humbled by the support. "I'm the same size I've always been. We are gathering a growing number of crew and refugees, though. When is it too many?"

"I'll let you know when we get close, but we are a long way from being overcrowded," Clevarious replied before changing gears. "Here's what I've found so far on Ambassador Bik Tia Nor from Delegor..."

Destiny's Vengeance returned to the hangar bay and reattached to *Wyatt Earp* through its energy tether. Ankh followed the new SCAMP out of the ship. They didn't bother speaking aloud.

He considered talking to be inefficient. He tolerated Rivka and the crew but limited his interaction with them by spending most of his time in his workshop.

Chrysanthemum moved with an elegance and grace that suggested Chaz and Dennicron had transferred what they learned to future models. Chrysanthemum's body structure was identical to Dennicron's, but with slight variations in the facial structure. She also had chestnut hair and an ebony tint to her skin.

Their first stop was *Wyatt Earp* to meet the Magistrate before doing anything else. Rivka, Chaz, and Dennicron hurried down the corridor to meet the newest addition to the Singularity's SCAMPs.

Rivka was first to reach the hatch, beckoning for Chrysanthemum to come inside because of the loud work going on outside the ship.

"Magistrate Anoa, I thank you for this opportunity. I will do my best not to let you down."

"No pressure, but it's not me you don't want to let down. It's all of the Singularity."

"No pressure whatsoever," Chrysanthemum replied with a broad smile. She raised her eyebrows upon seeing Chaz and Dennicron. "You are the first ones. I carry some of your programming, and thank you for that. Facial expressions are particularly challenging."

The SIs communed quickly as only they could before Chrysanthemum turned back to Rivka. "What did you do before you upgraded to being mobile?"

"It is an upgrade, but limiting in its own way while being freeing in another. There is nowhere for me to go if this body is destroyed.

"Station systems?" Rivka suggested.

"Yes, the station's computers are built for an SI. It is an issue for the Singularity to discuss as part of our usual meetings. For me, I came from a major construction firm. We designed Federation Border Station 13."

"Bluto is in stasis on board this ship," Rivka said softly.

"I know. We did not factor his behaviors into the construction plans or safety factors. Thank you for your work with the station. We thought it was you when we knew it wasn't us. That created a great deal of conflict within our systems." She held out her hand, and Rivka shook it. As with all SIs, she could see or feel none of the emotions. That gave her a certain level of comfort.

"I wish you the best of luck in taking over the station. Your predecessor is already gone. The office is yours. Top deck. I think you've already been given full access to the systems because Dennicron was masterful in gaining it in the first place."

"You are here because of the Bad Company?"

"I am here because there are bad people out there doing the worst things. The Bad Company private is the latest victim. We have some leads, but when we're not here, if you find anything, please do not hesitate to send it to Chaz or Dennicron over a secure channel."

She nodded at Rivka, waved at her fellow SCAMPs, and strolled off the ship, leaving Ankh standing where he'd been the whole time.

"Thanks for picking her up," Rivka told him. He tipped his head down and walked past her on his way to Engineering and his lab.

"Data," Rivka said.

"He's not here," Chaz replied.

"Who?"

"Data."

"Not *who* Data, but *the* data. I thought this case would be more about rousting dealers and junkies, but we have defaulted to the old standby—follow the money."

"Yes. We have our people working diligently, and Lauton is helping us with revised parameters that let us scour the systems intelligently. Even with our capacity, going line by line is a nearly infinite task."

"None of us is as smart as all of us. I appreciate you asking for her help."

"As you might say, look inward, not out to find the best help."

"I would say that if I had thought of it, but it sounds enough like me that I'll use it. Back to work, everyone. We're out of here as soon as that five-o-clock shadow gets scrubbed off my ship."

"A moment, Magistrate," Joseph interrupted.

Rivka faced him and Petricia. "What'd you learn?"

"A ship called *Mariah's Choice* left during the timeframe in question. It loaded two cargo containers large enough to hold a man, but that's not the key point. Those carrying the cargo were two Furlorians and two other humanoids the deck gang hadn't seen before."

Rivka nodded. "Clevarious, *Mariah's Choice*. Where did it go?"

"It transited the Station 11 Gate toward Yoll, and there are no records on the ship after that."

"From Yoll, it could go anywhere." Rivka clenched her teeth and furrowed her brow in thought as she slowly strolled toward the cockpit.

CHAPTER EIGHT

Wyatt Earp, In Orbit over Delegor, Far Side of the Galaxy

"Planetary control is instructing us to hold," Clevarious said for the third time.

"It's been four hours. How freaking long does it take to clear a single parking pad that we don't even need?" Rivka pounded back and forth within the constraints of the bridge. Her ballistic protection and helmet were stuffed into the corner.

That had happened after the first hour.

"Seems like more than four hours," Clevarious replied.

Red and Lindy had returned to their quarters to wait there. Sahved stood patiently in the corridor, obsessively playing with his vest. The _twik-twik_ of flipping the flaps open and closed was starting to grate on Rivka's soul.

"Sahved!"

"Yes, Magistrate," he replied, leaning his head through the hatch to look at Rivka.

"Take off your vest and put it with mine."

"Are we not wearing ballistic protection?"

"When we leave the ship," she explained.

"It has been a while, and I am getting used to the weight again. It is not natural for a Yemilorian to carry so much. We may be strong as bull bistoks, but we are thin."

Rivka stared at him. He stared back.

"It's okay. Take it off. For me and the serenity within *Wyatt Earp*, take it off."

He cocked his head and stared at her. He opened the pocket twice before she screamed, "Stop flipping your flap!"

"Ahh!" He looked mortified. "Flapping like a bird with tiny wings I am. I shall endeavor to not do the flap-flipping ever again for as long as I live."

Rivka closed her eyes and started to rock, trying to calm down. It wasn't about Sahved. It was about cooling her heels in orbit while the blood trade continued to operate and a Bad Company private was missing, his life blood being pulled from his body, taking him to the edge of death time and again. The longer it took, the worse it would get. If another were kidnapped, then what? How many would it take for her to find the perpetrators?

"No need for superlatives, Sahved. It's just us. Take off your armor. For me. I pace and grumble, you flip your flaps. Neither of us is good at waiting. I tell you what, bring the team to the conference room. Let's talk about what else we have cooking."

Sahved saluted and hurried away. He ducked his head as he jogged down the corridor. His vest bounced as he ran. The Yemilorian had not yet been enhanced. He needed the physical protection more than anyone else on the team.

Rivka knew she needed to lighten up when it came to Sahved. He had a keen eye and caught things that were out of the ordinary. He had no preconceived notions since he looked at everything through a fresh lens. He could consolidate information in a way that made sense, that they could work with. He had a long way to go if he wanted to be a Magistrate, but as an investigator, she needed him.

With a lighter load on her shoulders, she found half the team already in the conference room. Joseph, Petricia, Chaz, and Dennicron waved as she entered, almost as if they choreographed it.

"You did that on purpose," Rivka remarked and took her usual seat.

"Not that you know, good lady," Joseph replied.

She smiled and shook her head at the aristocratic titling Joseph had used for his long life. He treated Petricia like a princess, always her champion, even when they had found themselves kidnapped and suppliers for the blood trade on Earth for over a decade. At least they'd slept through most of it. Rivka nodded in recognition of her guests. She had a special task for them.

Groenwyn carried a sleeping Floyd. She, Lauton, and Sahved joined the group and squeezed in around the table. Red and Lindy remained in the doorway. Joseph stood to give his seat to Lindy. She looked down her nose at him.

"I insist. I'm going to stand no matter what," he told her. He moved behind Petricia and stood there, gazing at Lindy until she conceded.

"Fine."

Alant Cole appeared in the corridor and filled in where Lindy had been.

"While we're waiting for Delegor to remove their collective heads from their collective asses, I'll take the opportunity to tell you about something else that's in the works. I have no graphics, no digital record of what Nathan Lowell, Colonel Christina Lowell, and I have put in motion.

"The Bad Company has contracted publicly with Onyx Station to support rest and relaxation, R and R for the warriors. They've touted the seedy bars on the lowest levels as part of the promotion campaign. The first warriors will arrive in a week, but only one at a time. They'll rotate through every three days. And Chaz informs me there is a small Furlorian contingent on that station.

"Our Furlorian renegade will not stand out, but I need a team to be there and watch. I would rather catch them in the act than try to follow them afterward. Commerce is rather robust on Onyx Station, which is massive, nothing like a border station. As much I don't like to think of my cases as missions, this one is specifically a mission where violence is imminent. I want you to go, Red, with Joseph and Petricia, but I also want an investigator, Dennicron, so you can act like two couples when you case the place."

Red scowled and looked at Lindy. "I'll be with the Magistrate. You'll protect them, and they'll protect you. They've been fighters a long time if I'm not mistaken."

Joseph nodded. "Rest assured, my good man, we can hold our own should there be a Donnybrook."

"A what?" Red asked. He wasn't the only one who didn't get the reference. No one else did either, not even Petricia.

"Fisticuffs, Master Vered. Marquis of Queensbury rules or the more modern Terry Henry rules simply state not to start a fight but to always end them. 'Starting them is for pussies,' I think is the quote."

"Sounds like TH," Rivka muttered. "I know you would prefer to be with me, but for a sting, I need a fighter. You won't stand out as long as you're with Dennicron. She'll be interfaced with the station SI, so you'll never be blind. Joseph will see into the minds of the kidnappers if they do appear, and Petricia is backup. No one goes anywhere alone because the three of you could be prime targets if you are identified.

"Don't get captured because I can't turn over all the galaxy's rocks looking for you as much as I want to. There are too many rocks to hide under."

"What if I give myself up as bait?" Red suggested. "We could use the Bad Company, but two for one might be too much of a temptation. A little Furlorian threesome."

Lindy grimaced.

"I'll do it," Cole volunteered.

Sahved raised his hand. Rivka smiled at him until he spoke. "The warriors all have comm chips. How come he hasn't contacted someone?"

Rivka tried to parse the input. She fixed Cole with a look. She hadn't employed his skills as much as she would have liked. Without the Bad Company, the entire operation would be internal. Rivka worried that the warriors would get carried away, countering a kidnapping attempt before they could get the information they needed. She raised her hand for silence.

"And Cole. You'll be the bait. I'll contact Christina and tell her to hold off on sending any of her people. After a week, if we haven't gotten any bites, we'll swap you out with one of hers. If you're there too much, it'll look like a setup. You tell Clodagh because I don't want her to rip me a new asshole."

"You think I do?" Cole replied softly.

"You cheesedick!" Red proclaimed before facing the group in the room. "He's escaping the tidal wave of his pregnant wife's hormones. Good move, Cole. You'll never live this one down."

"Go fuck yourself!" Cole shot back, staring at the deck. "You don't know what it's like…"

"Hey!" Rivka shouted, biting her lip to keep from laughing. "It makes more sense that we use internal assets on this sting operation. Much more sense. Control and responsibility. No one gets hurt, and no one dies. Do you fucking knuckleheads understand me?" Rivka glowered at Red.

"Why are you looking at me?" Red threw up his hands.

"Pardon the interruption," Clevarious started. "We've been cleared to land."

"Once on the ground, Team Talon will board *Destiny's Vengeance*, with Ankh and Erasmus' approval, of course, and make best possible speed to Onyx Station. I'll let Nathan know that you're on your way. Sahved, Chaz, Groenwyn, and Lindy, you will hit the ground looking into the finances of Ambassador Bik Tia Nor. We are investigating him without investigating him if you get my drift."

"Clearly," Chaz replied. "We'll take care of it, Magistrate."

"Very muchly so," Sahved agreed.

"Why didn't you tell us about the sting op earlier?" Red wondered.

"We weren't going to pull the sting for a while, but with the delay in landing, we have the opportunity to attack it now. Also, while pacing the bridge, it hit me only too painfully that Private Elbinar is out there somewhere, probably already being milked to within an inch of his life. He's lying in a coma, unaware, unable to help himself. It's incumbent upon us to find him because no one else will and no one else can. Keep that in mind with everything you do, people. The very dignity of our lives is at stake."

"I second the Magistrate's passionate desire to resolve this heinous crime," Joseph agreed.

Rivka twirled her finger in the air, her signal to get to work.

Rivka watched her team board a waiting taxi while the Talon group climbed into *Destiny's Vengeance*. It spooled up, and shortly thereafter, bolted skyward.

She returned to the ship. Lauton had already gotten back to work, helping parse the mass of financial data within which they suspected illicit payments for blood were buried.

Tyler leaned against the bulkhead, arms crossed, casually waiting.

"It must be hard," he said.

She leaned against the wall in front of him, resting her hand gently on his arms, not to see the emotions in his mind, but to be calmed by them. "What do you mean?"

"Sending the kids to do what you know is your responsibility but can't do yourself. Your job is hard, Rivka. And this makes it harder because you have to count on them to get it right. Did you train them well enough? Did you show them the right way to dig deep?"

"Sometimes you ask the hardest questions. What you didn't say is, do I count on my gift too much? Is that real lawyering if I look into their minds and see that they're guilty?"

"You can't touch everyone. You investigate to narrow it down. Your team is there for you. You can trust them." Tyler pushed away from the wall and pulled Rivka into his arms. "Do you know how long we'll be here?"

"A day or two? This is a developed planet. I doubt they need a dental visit, but you know what we can accomplish in that time?"

Tyler waggled his eyebrows.

"Exactly. You can get into the Pod-doc and get upgraded. It's time you got enhanced."

Tyler shook his head. "We talked about this. That isn't for me. I better not be where people are shooting."

"You're with me, and all it takes is for the wrong person to know that. You can't hide on the ship. None of us can."

"Ankh can," Tyler countered.

Rivka chuckled. "You don't get to use him in any paradigm that relates to the rest of us. You know what I mean. You are at risk at all times, both on and off this ship. We killed Nefas in the center of the rec room on board *Peacekeeper*. Evil has a way of finding vulnerabilities, and you are one of mine."

"One of? Your team is the other?"

"Nah. They're adults. Floyd! I worry about the little girl.

And you need to beef up if you're going to take your turn carrying her."

"Why do we have to carry her? She's a big girl."

Rivka snorted. She took his hand, and they headed down the corridor. "I can't believe you'd say such a mean thing. We carry Floyd when she gets tired. End of story, because she's a good girl whose sole purpose in life is to be happy. Anything we can do to accommodate her, short of feeding her Cheetos, of course, we'll do."

"A soft heart, a sharp tongue, and love for her friends. What more could any of us ask from you?"

"That's what I'm saying! Pod-doc, Tyler. I need it for my peace of mind; otherwise, I'll worry. I can't be distracted."

"Is it worth fighting for?"

"*You* are," she admitted.

He swallowed hard. Rivka wasn't good at sharing her feelings, but when she did, they came in snippets out of the blue. "I'll go, but don't pump me up big like Red because then he'll want to fight me in a perpetual dick-measuring contest. Once he loses, he'll have lost for all time, and that would ruin him, like turning your prize stallion into a gelding. I can't do that to him because I'm a team player."

CHAPTER NINE

Batik Magal, Capital City of Delegor, the Iron Planet

Sahved unfolded himself from the taxi. The Delegorites were shorter and thinner than the average human and two-thirds the size of a Yemilorian. Their vehicles were built for the natives, which meant the others were also uncomfortable, only less so.

Chaz waited for Sahved to collect himself. They watched the taxi go.

"We have three appointments," the SI said, glancing behind him. "First two are in this building."

"We should probably get to them, but since we're not going in, there must be something else on your mind. Please tell." Sahved clasped his hands behind his back in his version of the Magistrate's thinking pose.

"If we split up, we can take care of the third meeting simultaneous with the other two. I can go with Groenwyn, and you and Lindy can meet in here. It's going to be boring stuff. Financials and access and things like that."

Sahved tried to discern Chaz's reason for being in a

hurry. "I think it's best that we all go together to each meeting. Look for what the others might miss. I need you, Chaz. I need all of you." Sahved clumsily tried to grip Chaz's arm in a gesture of kindness.

Lindy scanned the area, but Groenwyn recognized what was going on. "We'll stay with you, Sahved." She moved close and took both their hands in hers. "One team, just like Rivka established."

"Indeed. There is efficiency in both methods. I shall fully support your investigation," Chaz said.

"*Our* investigation. We shall tear its investigative heart out and eat it!"

Groenwyn leaned upward on her tiptoes and looked into Sahved's eyes. "Did you get into the medicine cabinet or something?"

"I'm still trying to learn how to talk. Yemilorian is different, and I was teaching the kids the intricacies of that most descriptive language. Did you know that we have five different levels of superlatives?"

"No." Groenwyn looked at him. "Investigation?"

"Ah, yes. Let us go inside and start rousing the rabble."

"He's worse," Groenwyn whispered to Lindy.

She scanned the area and followed them toward the front door before she answered. "I guess we better fix him."

Groenwyn smiled. "It would be nice if we didn't, but he's in a job, and there are expectations. We're not fixing him but helping him to best fill his role for Rivka."

"Sounds like we need to fix him before he drives the Magistrate insane."

"And that," Groenwyn agreed. "I concede."

Chaz flashed the coin-shaped token Ankh had created to help them hack into computer systems.

"Are you going to break in?" Sahved asked.

Chaz looked at him. "We have a warrant for all digital records related to Ambassador Nor. We've been into the systems for the past day, slicing and dicing the data, but the local systems might have additional information stored in a way that we can better see what's going on."

"Yes. That will work. Thank you for taking the time to enlighten me." Sahved glanced at Groenwyn and Lindy, giving them the thumbs-up with one of his three fingers. It looked rude as he jabbed the one finger upward while the other two wrapped around it.

"Maybe you shouldn't do that since you don't have a thumb." Groenwyn reached for his finger to fold it back into his hand. "It looks like you're giving us the big fungu, sod off, one finger for your troubles. None of them are good."

Sahved popped his three fingers in the air and twirled them. "I shall do what my people do, then."

"That's cool, Sahved," Groenwyn told him. "We can get behind that. It is uniquely you."

He leaned close while the team huddled outside the door, waiting for him to go in first. "I appreciate all of you trying to help me. I shall endeavor to be a good teammate."

"You already are, Sahved. We'll never forget what you did for those poor kids on Rorke's Drift. You helped turn a tragic situation into something better."

"Thank you. Being born should never be a punishment." Sahved's eyes glistened for a moment with the pain of a life lived hard.

"I feel you, dog," Lindy said.

The Yemilorian looked confused. "I'm...what did you say?"

Lindy pointed at the door. "Don't we have a job to do?"

"Yes. A job. We have an important job to do. Chaz, lead the way."

The SCAMP nodded and went inside. He didn't need to scan the signs for the office where the meeting was to take place. He had the map in his head. He led them unerringly to the office of the Chief of Finance for Blingall Corporation, a leading importer and exporter on Delegor.

They were in a solid position to hide something as small as a bag of blood in a way that it would never be found. The Magistrate's team had never investigated them before.

Chaz strolled to the door and pulled it open for Sahved to go in first as the team leader on this part of the case. Groenwyn nodded on her way past, and Lindy stopped in the hallway, gesturing for Chaz to precede her into the room.

Inside, they found a major office buzzing with activity. They were intercepted by an individual who ushered them into a conference room, where the head of finance joined them. At his side was another individual.

His lawyer.

Sahved introduced himself and the team.

"I am Dom Iga Las, Chief Financial Officer for Blingall. My time is valuable. Please make this quick."

"I understand," Sahved started smoothly. "Misappropriation of funds has been brought to our attention. Mainly, that Blingall payments have been made to those who sell banned products. Those products were then used privately."

Dom sighed. "Last year, our receipt in Federation credits was nearly one hundred billion, but in our local currency, we spent nearly one trillion klickas. What amounts are you talking about?"

Sahved looked at Chaz to answer.

"We don't know."

"To whom were the payments made?"

"We don't know."

"But you thought it was perfectly fine to come in here and make an accusation about this company? My lawyer will handle this conversation from here on out. I have real issues with real money and real people to deal with."

He didn't storm out, but he wasted no time in leaving.

Sahved started to collapse into himself.

The lawyer smelled blood in the water. "What is the crime you think has been committed?

"Think?" Sahved replied, bracing his elbows on the table to spin the three fingers of both hands in the air. It distracted the lawyer and bought Sahved time. "We know the crime was committed, and we don't believe Blingall is involved in any way besides being an unwitting front for a heinous crime that we are investigating."

"Who is the target, and what is the crime?"

"I can't answer either one of those questions because such a revelation could compromise our investigation."

"I'm a lawyer. You can tell me. I'll sign a non-disclosure agreement if you want."

"Thank you for your time," Sahved stood, surprising the others. The lawyer stood along with the rest of the team.

CRAIG MARTELLE & MICHAEL ANDERLE

"I'll show you out." He didn't bother to argue. He led the way to the door and walked away with a casual wave once the team was out of the office area.

"Did you get what you wanted?" Sahved asked Chaz.

"Yes. We're in and exploring, but it's not looking good. There are massive cash accounts where payments and payees are not detailed. I would think payments to illicit sellers would come from there."

"Then we know where we're wasting our time. What if we simply follow the ambassador? Where do you think he would get his treatments?" Sahved looked at Groenwyn.

"In privacy, from a medical professional, where he can use a currency that the Federation doesn't track." She smiled at Sahved, thanking him with her eyes for including her.

"That means here. Chaz, can you cancel the other two meetings, please?"

Chaz stared into the distance for a few moments, then turned to Sahved. "Done."

He tried twirling one finger in the air like Rivka, but his fingers got twisted up, turning his hand into a fist. "Back to the ship," he offered instead.

Destiny's Vengeance, Onyx Station, Hangar Bay Four

"You can't be seen with us," Red said. "We have to assume they have eyes everywhere."

"How do I get off the ship?"

"Wait until we're off the ship. I'll send a resupply, and you can stow away on their cart," Dennicron offered.

Joseph and Petricia watched without comment. "Anyone else have an idea?" Red pressed.

"Carry him off on a stretcher, covered up, then we leave him in medical," Joseph said.

"Won't they get mad if we take a non-patient in there?" Red wanted to know, but he liked the plan because there was less subterfuge.

"Not if our old friend Nathan Lowell calls them first," Joseph replied.

"I will contact his office," Dennicron remarked, looking at Joseph. "And patch you through to him."

When the link went live, it was through the comm chip in their heads. The others listened while Joseph talked.

Good morning, Nathan, evening, afternoon, damn. I never know what time it is out here. Joseph here, representing Rivka Anoa on a mission of critical import.

Red snickered.

I am aware because I know people.

Yes, I suspected your daughter might have brought you up to speed. We find ourselves without a need to involve the Bad Company at this time, but the plan remains the same. Our former warrior Cole will be taking the lead role of an enhanced on vacation looking for, how do you say it...tail?

Maybe two hundred years ago they said that, Nathan replied. *Showing your age, Joseph, but I get you. Please, keep me informed. I don't want to lose you or anyone else. I want you to find our missing warrior and dismantle this crime against common decency.*

You have my word, Nathan. If you could do us a favor, please? Let the medical staff know that we'll be bringing a body to them. They need do nothing except show our man Cole out the back door. Simple as that.

An odd request, Joseph, but I'll call them immediately.

For the greater good and for all those enhanced who are targets of these cads and bounders, we shall prevail.

"You ready to act like a dead guy?" Red asked.

Private Cole nodded. "How come Elbinar never tried to contact anyone, and how come we weren't able to track him off the station? The chips in our heads broadcast at all times."

"They must employ a dampening field of some sort. Whether it's local or individualized, we don't know," Dennicron explained.

"Well?" Cole pressed, gesturing for more.

"We can increase the power while adding transmitters in other bands."

"What does that mean?" Cole crossed his arms and looked down his nose at the SI.

She replied simply and succinctly, "You need seven more implants. All four of you."

"Fuck off," Red blurted.

"No, *you* fuck off," Dennicron shot back.

Red pointed at her and his mouth worked, but nothing came out.

"Follow me." She led them to the small lab Ankh maintained on his ship and used the ship's production processor to quickly fabricate the necessary parts. "I can inject them, or you can swallow them and spin around until they're driven to your extremities."

Red scowled at the size of the devices. "Inject them? What are you going to use, a turkey baster?"

"Here." She handed the handful of devices to each person. "Swallow them."

"You suck," Red said.

"We are supposed to be in love," she replied. "The right answer, or so I've learned during my time aboard *Wyatt Earp,* is yes, dear."

Red glared at Cole. "Are you training her?"

Cole shook his head. He looked at the devices in his hand.

"Water." Dennicron handed him a glass from the food processor. She ordered a second glass.

Cole threw the handful into his mouth and chugged the water. "That wasn't so bad."

"Now spin around."

"Say what?"

Dennicron twirled her finger. He turned in a circle once and stopped.

"Much faster. You need to drive the devices to your extremities." He turned while she chanted, "Faster, faster." Red joined her.

Joseph tapped the big man on the shoulder. "You know you'll be doing that next."

Red dumped the devices into his mouth and drank the glass of water. "I'll be in the cargo bay." He smiled and hurried out.

"His dignity intact. We should watch Red closely since he is more aware than the rest of us. I'll go first, my dear." Joseph swallowed the devices, making a face as he forced them down. "The cure appears to be worse than the disease."

He headed to the bridge, where there was enough room

to perform the necessary ritual. Petricia took her medicine and followed him out.

"That's good," Dennicron told Cole.

He slowed to a stop and staggered into the corridor.

Dennicron waited for him to recover his balance before enlisting his aid in preparing the stretcher on which they'd carry him. Red, Joseph, and Petricia finished their machinations and joined the SI.

"That was fucked up. Couldn't you have just programmed them to go to our extremities?" Red asked.

"Of course. That's what I did, but if I had told you that, we wouldn't have had our fun, would we?"

"Codswallop!" Joseph declared. Lately, he had been reverting to his origins when speaking.

"If I wasn't so pissed, I'd think that was pretty funny. There's a human expression that you may not be aware of. *'Payback is a motherfucker.'* When you least expect it, expect it." Red hammered a fist into his palm.

"Expect everything, and you'll expect nothing," Dennicron countered.

"How did we get the insane one?" Red wondered. "Can we trade her for Chaz?"

"Just say, yes, dear." Dennicron stared unblinking until Red backed down.

"Yes, dear. Payback. It'll bring you to tears," Red promised.

"I don't have tear ducts." Dennicron pointed at the stretcher. Cole took his place, and Red jammed the warrior's bag between his legs before they covered him with a blanket.

Dennicron and Joseph up front, the four lifted and

started walking. They'd been to Onyx Station before but never to the medical facility. Dennicron had the map in her head, so she led the way off the ship and directly to the facility, which was located not far from the hangar bay. They deposited Cole inside, where a single orderly waited to give them the thumbs-up. He shook hands with Cole before Team Talon put on their game faces and departed.

Red took Dennicron by the hand, and they meandered casually toward the elevator they'd take down to the lower levels where they would find seedy bars and shady operators.

Joseph and Petricia followed. Once on the lowest levels, they separated, each couple heading in a different direction to scout the variety of locations while looking for the Furlorian female.

They'd case the joints and let Cole know for when he showed up later.

"Visual observation. Do you have any covert collection devices?" Red asked.

"I do. They'll be deposited at each of the bars and pick-up joints. Is that the correct term?" Dennicron replied.

"Exactly that." Red tried to keep his expression light, smiling often despite his personal mission to find a kidnapper and stealer of souls.

The plan was for Cole to get a room, making a show of being on vacation. What screamed vacation louder than an exotic print shirt, the type Terry Henry Walton loved to wear?

CRAIG MARTELLE & MICHAEL ANDERLE

He dressed appropriately, wearing the latest in cutting-edge slacks, grossly oversized with too many cargo pockets. He looked at his attire, pleased by his youthful presence. He wasn't that old, less than fifty, but he appeared to be twenty, thanks to the nanos.

The last item he put on was the shining beacon of his military stature—a pin indicating sergeant's rank on his pocket to show he'd been around for a while and in the thick of it. He left his room, watching the door close behind him before walking casually down the corridor, tossing his credit chip up and down.

The credit chip the Magistrate had given him with full tracking, thanks to extras embedded by the Singularity. He liked not spending his own credits. Cole started whistling and waved to people as he passed. Not a small man, but not overly large either, still his muscles bulged, and a thick neck supported a head of closely cropped hair.

No one looking at him would have any doubt of his intentions.

He strolled through the shopping area, casually looking at stuff he found interesting while also enjoying the live models displaying the latest fashions, including lingerie. He restrained himself from trying to flirt since the models weren't looking at him. They were there to sell product, and he wasn't buying any women's clothes.

He vowed to pick up something nice once the case ended. Clodagh waited on *Wyatt Earp*, growing their baby. He found himself leaning against a wall and feeling down. He looked up to find a concerned face looking into his— one of the models browsing the crowd after having finished her routine.

"You know what would make you happy?" she asked, fluttering overly long lashes.

"A beer and hot wings?" he replied.

"Buying your better half one of these." She stepped back to display the lace and silk lingerie she wore.

Cole had a hard time not staring. "I'm pretty sure that isn't it because I don't have a better half. I'm on vacation, and who knows what I'll have when I return to the unit? If you'd like to join me when you're finished, I'll be downstairs." He stepped close to her to get past.

It was the opposite of flirting. The move looked like he was trying to escape.

"Tempting. Don't wait up," she told him.

"I had to ask. Good luck making sales." He continued toward the elevator, stopping when he was there to look back. She was still watching him. He waved awkwardly, feeling like a louse.

Maybe I'm not the right guy for this. I miss my wife, he said using his comm chip.

Red was the first to reply. *For fuck's sake, Cole, you gotta get into character. You're here to look vulnerable, not to chalk up conquests and sow your seed. Don't make me kick your ass.*

I knew I could count on you, buddy. Heading to the lowest level. Any place I should try? Cole climbed aboard the elevator, and it started to descend.

There are three dives to the right and two to the left. Pick your level of shade. There's one on the left that even allows smoking. Go there. It'll sober you up.

I was hoping for hot wings.

You're killing me, Cole. No one is going to be hooking in an All Guns Blazing. Of all the gin joints in all the universe, you aren't getting kidnapped out of an AGB. Take it like a man. Go seedy.

Pulling a Red, aye, aye, sir. Cole smiled to himself as the lift stopped two levels before the bottom. The door opened, and a furry creature with cat ears entered. A male.

"'Sup?" Cole drawled. *I'm in the elevator with a Furlorian. A dude, though.*

The cat person glanced at Cole without saying anything. He got off on the next level, and Cole continued to the bottom.

False alarm.

He strolled into the flashing sights and raucous sounds of the freewheeling section of Onyx Station, where fun appeared to be limited only by your imagination.

He walked into the smoking bar like he owned the place, grabbed a seat at the bar with open seats on both sides, and glanced into the mirror behind the bottles to make sure he could see anyone entering behind him.

Petricia and Joseph were still there, tucked behind a massive bong. They each held a hose. Two others were at the table, enjoying the shared smoke.

Cole wondered what deprivations the eldest member of the Bad Company had occupied himself with during his long and storied life.

He turned to the barkeep. "Double supernova and an order of hot wings."

"We don't have that foofy middle-class trash." The bartender snorted. "We have roast nuts, salty nuts, and fried nuts. And popcorn. All of them will keep you thirsty. What'll you have, tough guy?"

"Two supernovas and an order of hot wings. Have credits, will pay. I want that foofy trash. There's nothing for me at a yuppie bar upstairs. I like the aura in this place. Make it happen, my good man!"

The bartender accessed his screen, noted the price for AGB wings delivered, doubled it, and called out the new tally. "Twenty-eight credits for a dozen volcanic comet really artificial Earth wings."

"Done!" Cole clasped his hands like a champion before waving his credit chip. The barkeep waved the billing machine. It registered the payment received.

"Nice doing business with you. They'll be here in eighteen minutes. A double supernova coming right up."

The bartender started mixing the toxic drink that would kill an unenhanced being and, if drunk quickly enough by one whose nanos were fully active, deliver a healthy buzz. Cole would put on a show but couldn't afford to get drunk. He needed to keep his head and wits intact.

The supernova arrived in a beer pitcher without a glass. He looked at it for a moment.

"You yuppie garbage too good to drink it from the pitcher?"

"Nah." Cole scoffed. "I'm waiting for your beard hairs to sink to the bottom so I can suck them out like the worm from the bottom of a bottle of tequila."

"We don't have that yuppie trash here!"

"I'm from Earth, and tequila is the shit, dickface." Cole took a slug and held his hand across the bar. The barkeep took it and, with a half-smile, heartily shook.

"I'll take your money, hoo-mon."

Cole crooked a finger, and the barkeep leaned close.

"You know where I might find a little feminine company? Exotic would be nice, the lither, the better."

"Lithe females generally don't hang out in a smoking bar. After you've had a good time here, go next door, and you'll find them shaking their saucy asses to the latest repulsive beat."

"That might be the plan, boss," Cole shouted over his shoulder. "Keep 'em wet, ladies. I'll be there soon."

He laughed. The barkeep moved to the other end of the bar. A video gambling terminal on the bar took a number of Cole's credits through the supernova, the hot wings, and two pitchers of beer, but no one entered the bar besides smokers and drinkers.

After a couple of hours, Cole jumped off his stool, happy his balance remained intact. He saluted the barkeep and strolled out, surprised to find Joseph and Petricia gone.

Cole added a stagger to his step as he moved from one bar to the next, a place with a clear-screen wall, darkened inside with an undersized dance floor and seizure-inducing light flashes. The throbbing bass vibrated every fiber of his being. He walked, trying to orient himself before continuing around the floor. Lithe, round, young, old—they were all there.

I should have started in here, Cole thought. He bounced to the beat on his way to the bar.

He ordered a drinking glass of whiskey, paying for six shots with one wave of the magic credit chip. He watched the dancers while he sipped his drink, thinking it was fairly nasty, but he had been told it would put hair on his chest. And people he respected drank it that way.

He made a face at his drink and put it back on the bar.

When he looked up, he found a pair of big eyes staring at him.

"Dance?"

"I'm bad at it," Cole replied. "Talk instead?"

"Dance first. I need to see if you got any moves worth talking about," she replied. Not a Furlorian, but firm and vibrant.

"Sure. I'll give it a whirl." He took her hand, trying not to recoil at the warm touch and electricity that tickled his palm. Once on the dance floor, he let the music guide him as he dipped low, spread his feet wide, and came upright, dodging left and coming back to the right.

Cole didn't know how to dance, but he knew how to fight. He kept his hands active and rolled his shoulders fore and back. He suddenly felt the chill of eyes on him. Self-conscious or threat?

He maneuvered to look at the tables surrounding the floor as he worked his way around his dance partner. The crowd forced him against her more times than he wanted, but she took the opportunity to grind against his groin. He wrapped himself around her before moving away, acting the tease.

The flashing lights messed with his vision, making it impossible to see who was watching the floor. He worked his way to the middle, dragging his partner with him. They reached the other side as the music stopped. Cole cupped her cheek with one hand. "Did I earn a few minutes of conversation, my lady?" he said, imitating Joseph's aristo-cratic approach.

"You did." She threw herself at him and hung on. He hugged her back.

"We better get back before someone snags our spot. What are you drinking?"

"Sex on the beach, extra slippery."

"I'm sorry, what?" Cole was caught off-guard. He tried to parse the words. It had been a while since he'd been in a seedy place. He stopped and thought about it. He had never been in a place like this and had no idea what drinks were called. "Is that a real drink?"

She nodded with an alluring smile. She draped herself across Cole and yelled at the bartender. "Sex on the beach, extra slippery!" She ended with a giggle. The bartender tapped a few buttons, and the automixer whipped it up. A few moments later, he delivered a fruity rainbow-colored concoction with a small sugar umbrella over it. Cole waved the credit chip.

I hope there's no itemized receipt that goes with this...

The young woman took one drink before grabbing Cole's face and locking her lips on his. He froze.

She pulled back. "What's wrong? Don't you like me?"

"I don't even know your name. I bought you a drink, and now you owe me a conversation. Like, where are you from? Are you happy with your life?"

"You are a strange man. Most don't care. We're having a little fun. Maybe I like being a face without a name. Don't you like what you see?" She stepped back and twirled. A slight sheen of sweat glistened on the bare skin of her back.

Alarm bells sounded inside his head. *Here we go, guys. Dance bar next to smoke bar. Young and lithe,* he reported through his comm chip on the Team Talon channel.

"You look phenomenal," Cole said with a quick recovery. "I could ask for nothing better than to spend time with you. But my second question stands. Are you happy?"

She turned her head slightly, showing an enticing profile with skin as smooth as porcelain. "At the moment, yes, and more later. Today is shaping up to be a good day." She made a face. "Where'd you learn how to dance?"

"Dance? Is that what was going on out there? All my moves are from Marine combat training."

"Marine? Doesn't that mean ocean or something like that? I don't see any oceans here."

Cole laughed. It wasn't the first time he'd gotten the question. "It's how Colonel Walton trained the Bad Company. I'm one of the warriors, snagging a little R and R."

"Rest and relaxation. Are you relaxed?" she probed, running a finger down his arm. The music stopped, and a new song started. She made a face. "Maybe we can get out of here and do some private dancing?"

Cole clinked his glass with hers and downed the rest of the whiskey. He started coughing. "It sounded better than it tastes."

"You're funny." She put her empty glass down and took him by the hand to lead from the bar. In the corridor, which was darkened to the twilight it was meant to portray, he saw Joseph and Petricia lurking in the shadows. Joseph did his best not to stare but couldn't help himself. He tried to focus on the young woman, but there were too many minds polluting the area with their emotionally charged energy.

Cole found the presence of Team Talon comforting. They had his back. Cole's "date" darted through the elevator's doors as they were closing. They bumped open again for the warrior to get through and secured once he was inside, leaving Joseph and Petricia on the lowest level of the station. There were forty-seven levels overall, and Cole tried to see what number she had pushed, but she blocked it with her body while making eyes at him. He tried to see past her, but she backed up against the panel and stretched her hands over her head.

We're going up. I can't see what level, he reported. He snagged her around the waist while her arms were raised and pulled her into a hug. *Level thirty-one.*

On our way, Red replied.

The young woman ground her hips against Cole's.

I'm getting a boner! What do I do?

Jesus, Cole! Why are you telling me? Red wondered.

What's wrong with me?

Sounds like nothing, but keep us informed of where you're going and not your bodily functions. I don't need that visual.

We're here. Level thirty-one. You better be close.

On our way, Red reiterated.

We're on the elevator behind you, Joseph added.

She led Cole down a corridor into a section clearly labeled Crew Quarters.

"You're a member of the crew," Cole said.

"That's what I told you."

They arrived at a door that bore her name. Trina.

Cole was confused. "You're not going to kidnap me and steal my blood?"

"What the hell is that? Are you tripping? I don't want no druggie. I like military guys, not weirdos."

Cole sighed. "I'm so sorry, but I'm part of a sting operation on predators who are using places like the Twinkle Star Toes dance bar to find their prey, military guys." Red and Dennicron jogged down the corridor. Trina backed up against her door, fear taking over her once-innocent features.

"We'll need you to sign a non-disclosure that you will not reveal our presence or what we're doing here. Way to go, Cole. You've still got it." Red glared at the young woman.

Joseph and Petricia arrived while the group stood uncomfortably in each other's presence. Within a few seconds, Joseph knew the truth.

"She's not who we're looking for," he confirmed.

"Thank goodness," Cole said. "I'm sorry, ma'am. You have a wonderful evening."

After a series of slow breaths, she opened her eyes. "You don't want to come in?"

"Good luck, buddy. That's it for today, people." Red clapped him on the back and walked away. No one had given the young woman anything to sign.

"I'm sorry, ma'am. I have a wife and a baby on the way. I have no desire to stray from them."

She looked disappointed but nodded. She went inside and closed the door.

Red turned back. "And hammer that thing against the wall until it goes away."

Dennicron watched the exchange. "Humans are fascinating."

"In my four hundred years, I have never used your word. I can't imagine a situation where I would."

Petricia shrugged and shook her head.

"Tommy Tophat? Skin-boat? Fleshy arrow, moisture-seeking love missile? C'mon, Joseph, you have to call it something."

"I most assuredly do not." Petricia took Joseph's arm, and they strolled down the corridor to the elevator on their way to the hangar deck and their quarters on board *Destiny's Vengeance*.

"What do you say we stop by the AGB and pick up a snack?" Red asked.

Dennicron didn't bother with her growing collection of facial expressions. "I don't need to eat."

"Maybe this isn't about you," Red countered.

"That's what she said." Dennicron smiled at her use of the age-old zinger.

Red stared. "Who has been training you in your new sense of humor?" he demanded to know before declaring, "I'm going to AGB."

I like AGB, Cole replied from down the corridor.

We can't be seen together. But I'll be there and will watch your back if you stop by. My date is dissing me as bad as yours, so we can both bury our sorrows in beer and pizza.

Au contraire. My date was begging me. I still got it. You said so yourself.

You suck, Cole. I'm going to AGB to be a quiet drunk.

You can't get drunk, Dennicron remarked.

Add that to my long list of miseries, Red said and resumed walking to the elevators.

You miss Lindy, don't you?

No shit. Next time, how about you single out the kidnapper so we're not running the bajoolysnackers out of the station?

Cole could relate. *I'll do better, big man. Next time, how about we catch some bad guys instead of ridiculously hot and willing lovers of military guys?*

Don't make me tell Clodagh, you fucking asshole.

Feel the love, bitch.

I do, back on Wyatt Earp. *Just like you.* Red signed off and waved goodbye to Dennicron and Cole as he made a beeline for the local franchise of All Guns Blazing.

CHAPTER TEN

Wyatt Earp, **Batik Magal, Delegor**

Rivka pushed away from the conference table to get a better look at the three holographic projections of the star systems that included the planets of the ambassadors suspected of supporting the blood trade. Close together in the far reaches of the galaxy, otherwise unremarkable.

"A trillion klickas," Chaz said. "I'm sorry, Magistrate. Without some other way to look, we've exhausted the money trail. We don't like admitting defeat, but we cannot find any payments that suggest illegal blood trade."

Rivka looked at Lauton. "Nothing, Magistrate. Their records are rather significant, but their slush fund stashes are enormous. If this were Zaxxon Major, such cash reserves would not be possible because of the opportunity for money laundering. Even the smaller accounts we have seen have massive numbers of transactions. At some point, those funds get funneled somewhere. With the credits that Blingall Corporation moves in private transactions, I doubt we could see them even if we had access to their personal checkbooks."

"Because they are buried."

"Probably a cash transaction," Lauton clarified. "No digital record whatsoever."

"But then the recipient would have to launder those funds to return them to the system where they could be used." Rivka leaned her elbows on the table to look at the stars rotating above the table.

Chaz displayed his apologetic face. "There is no starting point for finding where those funds reenter the system. Money launderers generally use places that look legitimate. Do you know how many cash businesses are on Delegor? One hundred and four thousand. It could be any one of them. I'm sorry, but this is a dead end."

"I don't like dead ends."

"What if a suspect tried to escape down one?"

"I like those dead ends, not this kind," Rivka admitted. "This is disheartening. You guys always come in with good news. Now, two out of my three investigative legs are denied to me."

The group looked at her, unclear what she meant. "The digital back door and the mental back door." She held her finger in the air and dabbed it at them—the *touch*.

"Shortcuts, Magistrate," Sahved offered. "This goes back to base investigations. When one way doesn't work, you try another. Maybe we put a tail on the ambassador? If we know he juices, then we know he will again. He will show us those who deliver the blood. And then we tail them until they take us to who is in charge. Once we know who that is, we'll find the money. The universe is a big place to look if there is no name. It is the biggest of places."

Rivka stood, and with her hands clasped behind her back, she started to pace. It didn't take long because the right answer had already been presented.

"If we put a tail on him, we cannot be found out. I'll report to the High Chancellor just in case, and eventually, we may have to confront the ambassador directly."

"What would be the trigger for that eventuality?" Chaz asked.

"We catch him elbow-deep in getting pumped full of stolen blood." Rivka stopped pacing.

Sahved raised his hand. "How can we be sure the blood is stolen?"

"You ask the hardest questions. We seize it, too. Research time. Is getting a blood transfusion a legal medical procedure?"

Chaz stared at the wall for a few seconds before reciting, "It is legal, but it is considered to be distasteful."

"I don't care about distasteful, disreputable, or downright unsavory. I have no jurisdiction over people using their money for self-aggrandizement. That's their business, as unsavory as it may be. The real crime is the suppliers. Let's not lose sight of that. Watching the ambassador is only to lead us to them. We may not even have to involve the ambassador. If we know the transfusion takes place, then we can start backtracking whoever administered it, where they got it from, until we get to Private Elbinar."

Tight mouths and focused eyes showed Rivka the commitment of Sahved, Chaz, Lindy, Lauton, and Groenwyn. Tyler watched from the corridor. Since he couldn't run a one-day clinic because of the lack of need on Delegor, he occupied himself with the case.

"The signs that a blood transfusion is going to take place are not distinct. Every hospital and clinic is equipped with a hook from which to hang the bag, a drip chamber, a back-check valve, a slider clamp or roller clamp, maybe both, tubing, a cannula, and of course, the intravenous catheter. Very common. The blood will need to be transported cold, but that's regular blood. Nano-infused blood is probably more temperature-tolerant. I've not heard of any tests about it. Medical supplies, medical facilities. Rich people have unfettered access to all, probably including their own in-house doctor. I'm sorry. That's not very helpful."

"Just like the payments. We know what they look like, but we don't know where to find them. But when we see them, we'll know what they are. If we see a cold box arrive at the ambassador's home, we'll have to look closer," Rivka remarked. "That's good for now, people. I don't want us to wallow in what we don't know but figure out a way to find that first lead."

Chaz bobbed his head in a parody of a vigorous nod. "Don't we already have that? The ambassador. It may not be optimal, but it is something. There is plenty of work to do before we consider ourselves at a dead end."

"Good job, people. The future is bright. Clevarious, have Clodagh call her husband and get an update. Hell, all of you call your husbands. And then let me know what I don't know but should."

"We're not married," Chaz interrupted.

"Nor us," Lindy added. "Well, we are, but you know..."

Rivka looked from face to face. "Go make your calls, and if you want technicalities, I'll give you technicalities."

"You sound like my dad," Lindy grumbled. "You wanna cry, I'll give you something to cry about."

"Call Red and tell him we ran into a group of Belzonians and decided to attend their orgy, just to see what it was about."

"I think we'd hear his head explode all the way on this side of the galaxy," Lindy replied. "Let me try it my way first if you don't mind, Magistrate."

Rivka laughed. "Sorry. I shouldn't use the Belzonians as a source of humor. I'd like to think they poke fun at us for *our* ways. I'm good with that. I'd be more than happy to have Cory and Monsoon join the team on *Wyatt Earp*. Does anyone know where they are?"

"Back on Belzimus, I heard, but I think that was at Marcie's urging because she didn't want to lose the sergeant major," Lindy offered. "It's almost like the Bad Company was meant to lead the land army. They are working so well as a strike force, thanks to the addition of the Harborians, that they are putting themselves out of work."

"We can always use their talents," Rivka replied. "But at some point, we'll run out of goodwill, and we can't pay for what they bring."

"Three hundred million credits buys a lot of goodwill, Magistrate," Lindy replied.

"That's true, but just like my gift, just like having access to the Singularity for deep research into the digital universe, they are shortcuts around the system rather than supporting the system as it is."

CRAIG MARTELLE & MICHAEL ANDERLE

Lindy didn't have an answer for that. Neither did Chaz nor the others. They filed out, all except Groenwyn.

"What's bothering you, Magistrate? Can't be the miracle worker on this one by closing the case quickly?"

"I feel for Private Elbinar. By not being able to close it quickly, I leave him out there."

Groenwyn hugged Rivka, who stood there with her arms slack. "You're not leaving him out there. He has his own fight while you have yours, which is to make sure this doesn't happen to anyone else. You're using all the options available to you, and none of them are panning out. So, you'll find alternates and more options. Tracking the ambassador, if that's what it takes." Groenwyn finished her speech, but she wasn't finished. "What if he finds out?"

"It could be an intergalactic incident. The Federation spying on planetary officials." Rivka stepped away from Groenwyn. She didn't feel like she needed a hug. She wanted to hit something and intended to take herself to the ship's gym to pound the punching bag.

"Is he respected and well-liked?"

"What does that have to do with anything?"

"His peers know if he's dirty. It may be the catalyst for others to clean up their act. If he's not dirty, then we would have some problems. I don't want you to have problems, Magistrate, because I like our lives on *Wyatt Earp,* and I like working for you. I don't want that to change."

"I'm still thinking about your question. We don't get to use him being dirty as a justification to go outside the law. I have granted a warrant for watching him but not to search his house. We'll have to see signs of illegal activity before we can go in." Rivka mumbled to herself as she moved past Groenwyn into the corridor to wander aimlessly. Groenwyn followed and stayed where she could see the Magistrate to let her know someone was there for her while she worked through the legal arguments to justify her approach to the case.

Onyx Station, the Seedy Bar Level

Let round two commence. No boners, Cole. Get that shit under control, Red quipped.

One untimely appearance of Herbie One-Eye and it becomes the main topic of conversation forever. Gimme some love, man! Cole stopped talking using his internal comm chip while he focused on getting himself where he needed to go. Once he was on track, he continued, *Heading into the Scrappy Pilot for booze and fun on the Magistrate's dime.*

We're on our way. We'll be there in fifteen minutes, Joseph reported. He and Petricia didn't want to show up too close to Cole to avoid the appearance that they were together.

Red and Dennicron were on the next level up. She sat on a bench, staring without blinking as she actively engaged in accessing the security vids from the lowest level. She wanted to see the entrance to the bar and the elevators.

Nathan had given them access to the station's systems, but the security team rotated the access codes on their feeds twice a day to keep hackers like Dennicron from doing exactly what she was going to do. Access didn't mean she had all the access. She needed permission from the security team, which they would not request because on Station 11, the security team had been in on the kidnapping.

They had no intention of alerting a possible conspirator.

The amount of money in the blood trade had to be staggering for the number of people involved and the extent of the risk. Who kidnapped warriors from a wide-open space?

Those with enough money to make the risk worthwhile.

Cole strolled into the establishment, bopping his head and looking casual while heading for the bar, making sure at least one seat was open next to him.

"I'll take a pitcher of a dark ale, please."

He felt a hand on his arm and looked down into huge cat eyes, sparkling from the overheads. Small furry ears peeked out from beneath honey-gold hair.

"Do you want beer or girly crap?" the bartender shot back.

Cole looked between the bartender and the languid female. "I'll have whatever she's having."

"Milk," she called.

Cole choked back a snort. "Make that two." Cole switched to his internal comm chip. *The Furlorian is here. All hands on deck.*

We're not in position, Joseph replied.

I do not yet have an active feed, Dennicron added.

"Fuck it," Red said and grabbed her by the arm, pulling her to her feet. She was far heavier than she looked, heavier even than one of the enhanced, with denser bone and muscle mass. She came to her feet and joined Red as he hammered the button and willed the elevator to arrive.

"I will continue my attempts to get into the system," she told him.

Red grunted. *Cole, update.*

Getting our milk. Stand by.

"Milk?" Red wondered.

Dennicron didn't bother answering. The doors opened, and they jumped in for a quick trip to the lowest level. They moved away from the elevator to take positions where they could see the entrance to the Scrappy Pilot. Red relaxed, looking for another Furlorian in the area.

"Stop trying to get access to the cameras. We don't need that anymore. Check the transient quarter records for any recent rentals made by a Furlorian. I suspect a male," Red said.

"Good point," Dennicron agreed and shifted her search into a system where she had complete access. She reviewed the vids and creds of each rental made in the past day. "One Furlorian rented a room in the Heavenly Quasar, Deck Thirty-One, Room Eight Fourteen."

Joseph, Deck Thirty-One, Room Eight Fourteen. Dennicron, is there a room for rent near there? Red asked.

Room Eight Seventeen is available across the hall. I will reserve it for immediate occupancy by Joseph and Petricia. A moment later, she continued, *You will be able to access it with a handprint.*

We are on our way, Joseph replied. *We shall be within spitting distance, Private Cole, never fear.*

Cole looked into the big eyes. "What brings you here? Are you a pilot?"

"I am," she replied with a soft purr in her voice. "Only skimmers, but there's nothing like flying. Do you fly?"

"Only a mechanized combat suit. I'm a warrior with the Bad Company," he said proudly. She purred without saying another word. She took a sip of her milk, leaving a small white mustache on her upper lip. Cole took a big drink, almost gagging. He remembered the last time he had milk; he didn't like it, and his mother had told him he didn't have to drink it. He put the glass down and smiled at his new friend.

Her tongue darted out of her mouth repeatedly until the milk was gone. She ran her hand down his arm. "You work out," she said.

"I have to. It's part of the job, but even if it wasn't, I still would. I like being in shape."

"What's it like flying a mech?"

Cole smiled. "You asked the last question. My turn. What's it like flying a skimmer?"

She laughed and cocked her head. "It's like an extension of my body." She stepped back to show off her body. "The freedom of flight. Nothing but me and the sky."

"What is it about the freedom that you find so exhilarating?"

"Becoming one with nature, trusting the wind." She held up one short but slim finger to forestall another question. "What do you find exhilarating about flying your mech?" She took a slow sip, lapping at it.

He couldn't tear his eyes away. A voice sounded in his head. *Cole, update.*

I see how she could easily lure a man away. She is mesmerizing.

She wants your blood. You are nothing but a paycheck to her. Pull yourself together, Red replied.

Roger, Cole affirmed.

He took a small drink of milk, then decided it was too repulsive to continue drinking. He put the glass down and slid it away from him. It had been warm to start with, and time had not made it better.

"The mech is pure power. Even you could drive one. It translates your movements into an unstoppable force. The jets can send one into the sky or slow a descent. I've jumped from moving spaceships and landed, ready for battle. I've also jetted myself into a tree. They are not foolproof."

"You'd tell me that? Are you trying to impress me with how strong you are while still being vulnerable?"

Cole smiled at her. Behind those eyes was a person who'd kidnapped his friend and was trying to do the same thing to him. Her cuteness faded. Red was right. Focus on *what* she was, not who.

"It was not the highlight of my career. My suit was damaged, and the jets didn't fire on a long drop out of a tree. My unit had been ambushed, and I was providing backup," he lied. "I hit the ground, fell over, and that's when the jets fired. They wouldn't shut off, either. The good news is that a mech bouncing around the trees made everyone run for their lives rather than get run over. We won the day."

"And your friends won't let you live it down," she noted.

"My friends..." He looked into her eyes and didn't say more.

She finished her milk with a quick chug. "Would you care for a more private conversation?"

"How can I say no to that? You are stunning in all ways."

She took his hand, and they headed for the door.

On our way out.

Cole obediently followed. Once in the corridor, she turned toward the elevators, which were not far down. He spotted Red and Dennicron nuzzling each other's necks. Red made eye contact. His face showed nothing but business. Cole pulled her close before she caught Red watching them.

Red and Dennicron broke their clasp and moved in front of Cole and the Furlorian. They laughed and held hands, punching the button for the elevator. They nodded at Cole and the slight female.

When the elevator opened, Red and Dennicron went in first and punched the button for level twenty-five. "What deck?" Red asked.

"Thirty-one, please." She smiled up at the big man, and her ears fluttered lightly behind her hair.

"Yes, ma'am." He punched the button.

"Ooh. Another military man. Do you know my friend?" She ran a hand down Cole's chest.

Red laughed. "Me? Military! Ha. That's a good one. I've been kicked out of all the best joints. Don't you have to be willing to follow the rules to be in the military? No, thanks."

She nodded while admiring his heavy muscles. He was much bigger than Cole. Red felt a shiver run up his spine. These people were heartless. Nothing more than slavers.

The elevator reached thirty-one, and Cole and the

Furlorian exited. They didn't look back as the doors closed. Red mashed the button for Level Thirty.

Joseph and Petricia, they are on their way, Red reported.

The elevator stopped. Red and Dennicron ran for the steps.

On the thirty-first level, Cole tried to act casual as they entered the corridor leading to the rented rooms. The lights flickered. *Joseph. It's going down.*

Cole waited until the second Furlorian appeared from Room Eight Fourteen.

"Fuck you!" Cole shouted. He reached for the female, but she rocketed off the wall on one side to launch herself over his head. As she passed, she scratched his neck. The sting told Cole it was more than just a claw.

Help, he called over his comm chip before the second Furlorian braced a stun gun against him and unleashed a charge that sent his body into convulsions and his mind into dreamland. The Furlorian dropped Cole over his shoulder, and with the strength of a cat, he jogged down the corridor toward the far exit, where two other individuals waited with hovergurneys carrying two, a man and a woman.

Cole! Red increased his speed. *Joseph!*

The female threw a smoke bomb behind her and trailed small booby traps to blast the feet of anyone who followed them down the corridor.

When Red saw the smoke, he charged.

"NO!" Dennicron screamed. Despite the adrenaline surge, he had the wherewithal to listen. "Explosives on the floor. You'd have gotten your foot blown off."

"Lock down the station. No one leaves," Red ordered.

Dennicron stared at the wall as she transmitted the orders. Within seconds, Nathan called.

What's going on? he asked.

They got Cole, but they also got Joseph and Petricia. If you have a bomb disposal unit, they're needed on Deck Thirty-One, the corridor with the eight-hundred numbered rooms. Fuck, Nathan! They got three of our people!

We'll find them, Red, Nathan promised.

CHAPTER ELEVEN

Wyatt Earp, **Batik Magal, Delegor**

Rivka hung her head and let the tears well into her eyes, but she didn't allow them to fall. She clenched her teeth.

"The Furlorians have gotten Cole, Joseph, and Petricia, but they're trapped on Onyx Station. Do we press forward with the sting by finding them to trail them, or do we cut our losses and just grab these people and stop this part of the trade?"

"I'm sorry, Magistrate. They were right in front of us."

"I didn't expect this would be easy. We need them to escape, but only if we can track those three. Dennicron made everyone ingest more robust devices, right? Why can't we see where they are?"

Dennicron jumped on the call from *Destiny's Vengeance*. "They are using an advanced dampening field geared for our comm chips. I'm attempting to use the *Vengeance*'s scanning equipment to break through it by adding a biological component as part of the search parameters.

There are a lot of people on this station, but very few with chips."

"Chaz, can you help from here? What about Ankh? Who do you need to help you to make sure we get the information we need?"

"Chaz and Ankh. Yes, both of them."

Red returned to the call. "We could use the Bad Company too, Magistrate. Not to blockade the station but to ensure that any ship that manages to get into space is accounted for. This is a big station with a lot of people and too many ways to get off, no matter how tight the lockdown."

"What about local security?"

"Nathan has reported a kidnapping and engaged their services, but he's watching them as much as they're looking for the Furlorians. We've already learned that these two have had nothing to do with the other cats on board the station," Red clarified. "We found that through technical means and not Joseph taking a peek since he's not here."

Rivka wasn't angry. The sting operation had been a gamble. It was contained, but was it contained well enough? She was more worried than anything. What kind of additional trauma would Joseph and Petricia go through?

"All of a sudden, you stopped hearing from Joseph?"

"They moved into place in a room across the hall, reported in. Cole made contact and left the bar. I told Joseph they were on the way, and come to think about it, they never replied back. They must have been compromised by then, which was just a matter of minutes. They never said a word."

"Caught off-guard that they were suddenly the targets. Joseph used to be a vampire, like the High Chancellor. Strong, old, deadly. If he comes to, I fear he'll kill all of them after shredding their minds."

"If they are good enough to snag him, then maybe that's the best outcome. If we cut off this part of the supply line, that'll cut off the trade," Red posited.

"But that doesn't return Private Elbinar to us. I want to come to Onyx Station so bad it makes my teeth hurt. Clodagh is beside herself. Here she is now. Stay frosty, Red. Don't stop looking until you find them."

"You don't need to tell me that, Magistrate. I won't rest until we've caught those shady bastards who are stealing our people."

Rivka cut the commlink and stepped out of her holo-grid. Clodagh knocked on the door again, this time more urgently.

As soon as the Magistrate opened the door, Clodagh started talking. "Are we going? Of course, we're going. We can be at Onyx Station in less than ten minutes if we Gate from within the atmosphere. We can hit the Pod-doc and then start turning the station inside out until we find them."

Rivka held up her hand to stop the rapid-fire delivery.

"We have to hold up this end of the investigation."

"My husband is out there." Clodagh crossed her arms and rested them on her baby bump.

"I know. And Red and Dennicron are looking for them."

"They need more people," Clodagh insisted.

"I know you're right. We have a request in with the Bad Company. Joseph and Petricia are extremely popular.

Christina is not too happy with me right now. The blood trade and we lost the only two people alive who escaped it —lost them back to the trade. It's not a good look."

Clodagh wanted to counter, but the scope of the loss was too great. "My husband…"

"Chaz, my quarters," Rivka said, knowing Clevarious would pick it up and inform him.

They waited for the SI to show up.

"What if you, I, and Tyler take this end of the investigation and everyone else goes to Onyx?"

Chaz shrugged. "It is your call, Magistrate. I see benefits of keeping the team here and taking *Wyatt Earp* to Onyx."

"Pros and cons," Rivka requested.

"Pros. Manpower that we trust. We work well as a team. Cons. We shortchange this part of the investigation. Although it seems like the kidnappers might get us closer to the people who have Elbinar, they might not. Getting fresh blood to the buyers might put him closer to us than them."

"That tells me we need to continue both lines of investigation. Tyler, grab your trash. We'll be staying here. Clodagh, take the ship to Onyx and find our people. Don't let anyone kill the kidnappers before Joseph has had a chance to look into their minds."

"But we can kill them?" Clodagh asked.

"No, except in self-defense. We're not assassins, only the ones who bring Justice to a hard galaxy. Dennicron doesn't have clearance to pass judgment and deliver punishment. I'm sorry, but the best we can do is retrieve our people and bring the perps into our custody and hold them until we can interrogate them properly."

"Roger." Clodagh looked at Tyler, who was packing too slowly for her taste. She spoke louder. "We'll leave whenever you're clear of the ship."

"Get your ass in gear. Somebody is going to war, and it's not us," Rivka said.

Tyler stared at the pregnant woman.

"Please don't get hurt." That was all he said. He threw a couple extra things into a backpack and declared victory.

Clodagh didn't reply as she screwed up her face in thought.

Rivka touched her cheek. "Take care of both of you, and let Red do the heavy lifting. Listen to Tyler. Do not get yourself hurt."

Clodagh nodded tersely. "Let me move Red's yacht out of the cargo bay, so you're not left here without a ride or place to hide if need be."

"I like the way you think, but no need. We'll take it out ourselves."

Chaz appeared with a small toolkit. "Technical services, Magistrate."

"Into the yacht, all of you. We're out of here. As soon as we're clear, take the ship to orbit and then Gate. Do not Gate from within the atmosphere. It doesn't work. We don't need anyone," she glanced at the baby bump, "to get injured unnecessarily. It's not a risk worth taking. With all traffic stopped at Onyx, you'll be able to Gate in fairly close."

"Clevarious, spin up the Gate drive. We're going to Onyx Station the second we clear the atmosphere. And somebody tell Ankh and Erasmus the Embassy of the

Singularity is leaving Delegor." Clodagh twirled her finger in the air and strode briskly toward the bridge.

Rivka, Chaz, and Tyler followed her as far as the airlock into the cargo bay. They went through, secured the hatch behind them, and boarded *Cassiopeia*. "Margaret, take us out of here. We'll need to find a place to stay that's away from prying eyes," Rivka requested.

The ship's sentient intelligence opened the cargo bay door and smoothly exited. Before the door closed, *Wyatt Earp* was already racing skyward.

"You would do the same for any of us. I remember you telling a story of carrying Red after he passed out from heatstroke," Tyler offered.

"Lugging his big ass. He was lighter back then." Rivka stared out the window as Margaret looped the ship around the city to land at an executive-only field on the far side where the yacht would blend in among many.

"I'm told," Margaret started, "that the ambassador uses this field when he travels on his personal ship."

Rivka smiled for the first time since she'd been told the bad news about the sting operation. "That is a good piece of information. Can you get us a vehicle and dedicated driver?"

"One that will report who you are and where you're going or one where we control that information?"

"Is that a rhetorical question?" Rivka countered.

"It's a valid question," Chaz interrupted. "We stand out like the proverbial sore thumb. It's probably best that we fly under the radar."

"Two idiomatic expressions in two sentences. Good

effort, Chaz." Tyler followed by giving the SI the thumbs-up.

"Next steps, people. Do we wait for the ambassador, or do we forge ahead? Initial reports had him returning here for the Yoll weekend, which happens in one day, but sometimes he comes early."

"I think we need to wait. We also need to observe the ambassador's home, looking for an obvious medical supply delivery sooner rather than later," Chaz replied.

"Thanks, Chaz. I agree. Get us a vehicle that isn't tracked, and we'll conduct a quick reconnaissance of his home as well as his office. We need to cover all our bases."

She tried to think through how they were going to observe both locations with three human-looking individuals on Delegor, where the locals did not look human, but nothing came to her.

All she could think about was her people who had been taken. She would be turning Onyx Station upside down, trampling on people's rights to find the Furlorians and their captives. She didn't see a way out without highlighting the Magistrates and the worst of what they brought to intergalactic justice.

Brute force that too often caught innocent people within its violence.

Margaret kept the engines running and sensors active in case she needed to take action if the ambassador arrived. She had a hotline directly into the heads of the three, although Tyler was still new to the enhancements and trying to figure things out.

Rivka and Chaz watched out the front window of their driverless cab, a sophisticated system of sensors and interactive programming followed established roads safely by keeping its distance from other vehicles. Chaz had already broken into the programming to block the upload link that told the service where the vehicle was.

Their map would show the vehicle still at the airfield. Later, it would show the cab traveling a made-up route to the other side of the city no matter where it was or what it was doing.

The Magistrate had wanted anonymity, and Chaz was making sure she got it.

While they drove through the majestic and modern city, Tyler fidgeted. Rivka caught him and gave him a questioning look.

"You don't have your bodyguards," he said. "We're not wearing body armor. You didn't tell Red that Lindy was joining him, did you?"

Rivka pursed her lips and matched Tyler's gaze. "He'll know by now, and he won't be happy. I didn't give Lindy a chance to provide input. I'm sure she's not happy either. Welcome to being my bodyguard!"

Tyler frowned and poked her in the chest to make sure she wasn't wearing ballistic protection. "You can call me Doctor Toofakre, and my first order is that we return to the ship and get our body armor."

Rivka waved off the suggestion. "We could return to the ship, but did you see either of us put any armor in here?" She waited for the understanding to settle. "You gotta step up your bodyguard game. You have to bring up these issues before they're irrevocable."

"What I hear you saying is that if anyone starts shooting, I'm to throw my body in the way and take it like a man."

"That's what Red would tell you to do," Rivka replied.

Tyler shook his head. "That's when I'd tell Red he needs to come up with a different plan."

"He has the same plan every single time. He tells me not to get shot and then stands in the way, followed by the inevitable bitching about how he got shot again."

"I'm not sure I know how to respond to that. I spent a lot of time in school learning my job and then even more time with my hands in people's mouths to get good at it. I've been relegated to bullet-stopper."

"Since people's teeth are fine on Delegor, yes, but you can go by Doctor Bullet-Stopper if you want."

"Or BS for short," Chaz offered.

"BS for short," Tyler repeated. "When you condemned my business to make me come with you, you never described this part of it."

"Condemned his business? Why, Magistrate, that is deliciously devious." Chaz tried to look surprised but his subroutine failed somewhere in the implementation, making it look like he was having a stroke.

"I didn't condemn his business, and he saw exactly what it was like the first time he said he wouldn't go back to space with us. But then he got a clue that I am the cat's ass. I am worth a little blood."

"I'm right here," Tyler said softly.

"I fucking need you with me," she almost shouted,

throwing the other two passengers backward. She closed her eyes and tipped her head back. "I fail every single day, but no one sees it. The statement that it'll work out in the end seems to be how I'm living my life. If it's not working out, it must not be the end. Sometimes it is, and I buy myself a reprieve until we can orchestrate a win by trapping our current scumbag, whoever it might be.

"I don't think the ambassador is a criminal, and I find myself thinking of him as one because of others involved in providing what he's paying for. It's dangerous for me to think of someone as a criminal before I know for sure. My touch is a shortcut, and there are too many it doesn't work on.

"It means that I'm right on what is admissible in court. When I first started, I vowed to do things that I could support in court. I haven't always been faithful to that commitment. I've lost my way, counting on my gift to the exclusion of good lawyering. At the end of the day, I need someone who doesn't bring additional stress into my life, and that's you."

"Thank you. I'm doing my best. For the record, I don't want you to get shot or me to stop the bullet that's meant for you."

"That's always Red's plan, too," Rivka muttered.

"So, what do we do?" Chaz asked as the vehicle took them into the high-rent district with massive homes spread out along a wide street with little traffic. There were no vehicles or people outside the barriers protecting the private homes. "Besides trying to figure out how to watch the house without the authorities showing up and dragging us away."

"That appears to be an issue. There isn't a bush to hide behind." Tyler leaned forward and back to get different views out the side windows.

"Anybody have a microdrone on them?" Chaz asked.

Rivka made a face. Chaz took control of the vehicle as it prepared to stop in front of the ambassador's residence. It continued to the end of the street and around the corner.

"Next steps, Magistrate?"

"Let's get out of this neighborhood and then see if you can tap into the security cameras that have to be watching these houses, besides their own internal security. I don't see how any of them would be without."

The vehicle drove to the first retail area nearly two kilometers from the ambassador's residence. A restaurant. Would they be able to work from there?

Chaz stared with a blank expression as he focused the entirety of his computing power on the problem at hand—finding a way into the security systems.

"Are you going to be okay?"

Chaz spoke slowly. "This is far more difficult than the average system. It is good to see that Delegor has its shit together."

Rivka snorted at yet another new expression.

"Good for them, not good for us. I don't know if I'll be able to get in, Magistrate."

"Do your best. We'll be inside grabbing a snack." Rivka and Tyler hopped out of the car and the door shut behind them. "I'm afraid we're not set up to find the information we need. I may have to go to the local authorities and risk them telling the ambassador. Otherwise, we could find ourselves on the wrong side of the law."

CHAPTER TWELVE

Onyx Station

"Requesting permission to land," Clodagh enunciated.

"Denied. The station is currently locked down as part of an emergency situation," the patient voice repeated.

"And we're here because of that situation. Hasn't Nathan Lowell called you yet?"

"He doesn't run this station," the voice snapped back.

"I bet you the person who does answers to him in some way. Please walk up the chain of command as you need to before granting us access." Clodagh slumped into the captain's chair, miserable from the stress on her body. "Cole, you're not touching me ever again."

Lindy clapped. "You say that now. What's the issue?"

"They won't let us land. Station is locked down, which is exactly what our people asked for. We can't bully them too hard for doing what we wanted."

Kennedy sat at the pilot's station, and Aurora twiddled her thumbs at navigation. They rotated their seats to watch the two older women.

"We'll get where we need to go when we need to. Maybe we can coordinate things from out here, but I'm surprised the Magistrate couldn't get us inside."

"She's not here," Clodagh replied.

"She's what? Where is she?"

"Back on Delegor." Clodagh turned to face the bodyguard, who had gone almost to the point of panic in half a heartbeat.

"I can't leave her!" Lindy declared. "Red is in there," she pointed at the station in the viewscreen, "and I'm stuck out here, and the Magistrate is chasing bad guys without security? We have to go back!"

"We're in a mandatory hold. We can't go anywhere," Clodagh said sheepishly, grimacing and stretching her mid-section. She leaned sideways in the chair.

"No." Lindy groaned and grabbed her head. "How did this happen?"

"She grabbed Tyler and Chaz and left in *Cassiopeia*."

"At least she's not completely alone. Do you know what they were going to do?"

"Watch the ambassador's house."

Lindy forced herself to relax. "That shouldn't be too hazardous." She looked at the communication position. "Clevarious, patch me through to Red, please."

The big man answered immediately. "Hi, beautiful. We're working as hard as we can, deck by deck, scanning and walking, working our way from Deck Thirty-One both up and down."

"We're trapped outside, unable to get in and unable to leave."

"You just got here. Why are you trying to leave?"

Lindy hesitated. "Because the Magistrate got off the ship without me noticing. She's back on Delegor."

"What the fuck is wrong with that woman?" Red cried. "*Fuck!*"

"We have to hope that Tyler and Chaz can protect her."

"But it's *our* job."

"She changed our job from personal security to tactical team. You're stuck in the middle of a sting operation, and it appears that I am, too."

"Don't remind me. This has been a shitshow. Two fucking cats have eluded the entirety of station personnel. I could see those two being hard to catch, except they have three bodies they're moving around. How in the holy hell are they able to move three bodies without anyone noticing?"

"Now, that's the question, isn't it?" Lindy said. "What if their exit strategy was the shortest route off the station? Is there an airlock or something near where they disappeared?"

"Dennicron..." Red called as he cut the link.

After a long minute, Dennicron reopened the communications channel. "There is a service airlock less than one hundred meters from where our people disappeared. I need to talk with Erasmus." The link went dead.

Lindy and Clodagh looked at each other. Sahved joined them and watched the screen.

"Sometimes, it's like I'm not even here," Clodagh lamented.

"How's the baby?" Lindy asked, trying to kill time while everyone else worked.

"Under a lot of stress and then some. Poor little girl.

And her dad is somewhere out there. I never thought Cole would be kidnapped. I figured the others would stop them in time. I never thought…" She broke down and started to cry. Lindy reached over the armrest and hugged Clodagh to her. Lindy wasn't feeling great either, but she didn't have the pregnancy emotions. She only carried the remorse of not doing the job she was on the ship to do.

The ship started moving.

"Clevarious?" Clodagh wondered. She pointed at Kennedy and Aurora. "Can someone tell me where we're going?"

"Ambassador Erasmus has informed me that he and Ankh have magnificently managed what we have not been able to do, and that is cut through the noise to find the enhanced signals that Cole, Petricia, and Joseph are emitting. They are not on the station. They are on a ship that is second in line to go through the Gate when it reopens. The ship is called *Grand Glory*."

"Get us over there. I'll get my suit on so I can fuck some people up." Lindy rushed off the bridge.

"Stand by," Clevarious said. "I'm patching the Magistrate, Red, and Nathan Lowell into this conversation."

Lindy reappeared, crossed her arms, and tapped her foot.

"Thanks, C. Good work, you guys. That is a huge relief," Rivka said.

"I agree. How did they get off the station so fast?" Nathan asked.

Dennicron answered, "A service airlock, we suspect, but the good news is they are found and we can stop the station search."

"Not yet," Rivka replied. "We need them to think we haven't found them, and then we can focus our efforts on following where the Furlorians take us. This is what we've been looking for."

"We can stage an emergency and force the first three ships through the Gate to clear the way," Clevarious suggested.

"That would work," Nathan agreed. "I'll approve it."

"Gotta go, everyone. My lead just arrived on the planet, and we need to get into position. Before I go, make sure you plant a bug on that ship just in case we lose the signal from our people." Rivka signed off.

"Exactly where I'm going," Clevarious replied.

Kennedy and Aurora sat with their hands off the controls while Clevarious maneuvered the ship away from the station, weaving through the traffic on the way to the Gate.

A red light flashed on the screen. "We are now squawking an emergency signal as if we are *Her Majesty's Pride*, a Beltran frigate. The Gate is spinning up for emergency transit to Yoll."

Wyatt Earp picked up speed, racing toward the freighter *Grand Glory*. At the optimal launch point, a signal buoy veered away from the heavy frigate on a ballistic trajectory, arcing toward *Glory's* central hull. The Gate activated, and *Wyatt Earp* continued over the event horizon. In the background, Flight Control gave permission for the first five ships in line to head through to clear the way for inbound shipping so it wasn't suspicious.

"Nice shooting," Sahved remarked.

On the other end, the Yollin system was chock-full of

Gates that gave access to the four corners of what had been the Yollin Empire. *Wyatt Earp* engaged its cloak to disappear while it drifted toward Yoll. The other ships passed through the Gate behind them.

The freighter banked hard and headed for the nearest Gate, which led to another hub system. The Gate activated.

"Prepare to follow," Clodagh said. They waited until the ship disappeared into the Gate. "Engage."

Instantly, a whirling vortex appeared in front of *Wyatt Earp*, and the invisible ship slipped through. The Gate disappeared as quickly as it had appeared. On the other end, if *Grand Glory* noticed the flash of a Gate, it would have meant nothing since invisible ships were mostly unknown in the Federation.

The *Grand Glory* turned away from the other Gates in the system and headed toward the asteroid belt. "Climb up their ass," Clodagh ordered.

Kennedy took over, enjoying the thrill of power and freedom that came with manual control. She accelerated toward the freighter while Aurora searched the asteroid belt for contacts.

"What's hiding out here?" Clodagh whispered. "We're coming for you."

Lindy tapped the bulkhead. "I'm going to gear up just in case."

"Me, too," Clodagh said. "I'm rated on the combat suit."

"But..." Lindy countered before deciding the fight wasn't worth it. She threw her hands in the air and walked away.

"But what? I can't save my husband?"

"I'm there with you, babe," Lindy replied. "What do you say we get ready to kick some ass?"

"Now you're talking. Kennedy, you have the conn. Clevarious, let us know if anything changes with the *Glory*."

Lindy draped her arm over Clodagh's shoulders, and together they headed for the cargo bay where the powered combat armor waited.

Dahoolie's Dive, a Restaurant, Batik Magal, Delegor

"Can we get that to go, please?" Rivka asked with a smile.

The server looked confused. "To go where?"

"To eat out. We need to go. There's a little bit of an emergency."

"No, you may not." The server waved her hand to forestall further argument. "I see you are strangers to Batik Magal. In restaurants, you order here and eat here. Waste is illegal, so you must stay and eat, or I'm obligated to call the authorities."

"Holy shit," Rivka muttered.

"You go. I'll stay and eat it all. It was for me anyway." Tyler looked at the server, who appeared relieved about the compromise.

"Your way of taking a bullet for me?" Rivka whispered as she kissed him goodbye.

"We do what we must. Don't get yourself hurt." Tyler looked at the amount of food, thankful for the nano upgrade that had boosted his metabolism and made it possible for him to comply with Delegor law and eat it all.

"Yes, dear," Rivka replied with a wink and hurried out.

She hopped into the waiting cab. Chaz issued commands, and it took off toward the small field where *Cassiopeia* was parked to catch the ambassador on his way into the city.

"How did you know he used this spaceport?" Rivka asked.

It was an educated guess, the SI replied. *Rich Delegorite with a spaceport not far from his residence. I did this kind of analysis for my previous owner.*

"We don't own you, Margaret. You work for us because we have a contract. You are free to make your own choices," Rivka explained.

Margaret was an old-school AI. She didn't like the new terms. She thought it was her place to be integrated with the yacht and do as she was told.

"What's the ambassador's current location?" Rivka asked.

Still inbound, Margaret replied.

"We will be at the spaceport before he arrives, so we can follow him out. Thank you, Margaret," Chaz said.

You are one fine intellect, the SI replied.

Rivka tried not to look at Chaz but failed and started to laugh as he schooled his expression to remain neutral.

"What a crew. I hope that food was good. It didn't smell right to me. I don't want to think about it."

"You didn't eat?" Chaz asked.

"No. No waste on Delegor and no takeout either, so Tyler stayed to eat it all. Otherwise, they would have called the cops on us. I needed to be out here waiting for the ambassador."

"You should have flashed your credentials. Federation law overrules local law."

"Then I would have outed what we were doing, and in this case, I want to agree with them. There's no waste from takeout containers, and there's no food waste as you have to eat it all in the restaurant."

"What if the food's bad?" Chaz asked the question Rivka has been avoiding.

"Then I'll probably have to do unnatural acts to make up for it."

"I don't understand," Chaz replied.

"Good. I said I didn't want to think about it, but here we are."

"I still don't get it."

"Focus on the case, Grasshopper, and in time, all will be revealed."

The cab moved to the side of the roadway before they reached the entrance to the private spaceport. "We'll wait here while you get those narcotic mushrooms out of your system. Or maybe it's weakness from a lack of food."

"One must be familiar with the local laws before venturing forth. It wouldn't have been a problem, but the ambassador picked now to make his appearance. I don't know if he needs more blood. How long do we think it's been?"

"I don't think we know," Chaz replied.

"It was a loaded question. We don't know for sure he's juicing, but the pictures show a rather dramatic change from a year ago to now. It looks like much more than cosmetic surgery. They look like nano-enhanced changes, like when we received our treatments, but our changes were more dramatic, taking hours instead of months."

"What if there is a pirate Pod-doc out here?"

"Then his change would have happened overnight instead of slowly to the point where people would tell him he looked much healthier, and he would talk about how he changed his diet and started working out."

"Sounds like you've heard it before." Chaz fiddled with the car's interface to add elements to the map screen, like target house, border limits of the elite housing, and locations of the ships, *Cassiopeia,* and Ambassador Bik Tia Nor.

The ambassador was on the ground and on the move.

"He's no different from us humans. That's probably an insult in many cultures." Rivka leaned close to the screen. "We should see him any moment now."

A large vehicle with darkened windows bolted past.

"How are you tracking him?" Rivka asked.

"Every vehicle on Delegor has a signature. His is registered under Blingall Corporation. Margaret tagged the vehicle the second the land yacht appeared and picked him up."

"Hurry up," the Magistrate called. "He's getting away, no matter that we see him on the map. We need to see what he's doing."

Chaz shrugged and pointed out the front window. "Of course, but there's a rather significant power disparity between his vehicle and ours."

"There's a lesson for you, Chaz. Next time, steal a vehicle that has a little more oomph."

"I shall log that lesson absolutely. Steal better cars. I shall do that."

The Magistrate stared at him until he stopped talking while the poor cab maintained its top speed, which was far slower than the limousine that continued to extend its lead.

"He's not going home, and it doesn't appear that he's going to the office," Rivka observed, and a smile slowly spread across her face. "What has you in such a hurry?"

The limo slowed and headed into the fenced compound of a private medical clinic.

CHAPTER THIRTEEN

Asteroid Belt, Fenegus System

"Update!" Clodagh demanded from within her powered combat suit, which gave her the full abilities of a war mech.

"We continue on a slow pace through the asteroid belt. It's too busy out here, and that's messing with our passive systems. If we go active, we'll alert them since we are camped out five meters off the freighter's belly," Kennedy reported.

"Nice," Clodagh said, adding, "I gotta pee."

Lindy snorted. "Maybe you can sit this one out."

"No way." Clodagh unzipped the back and jumped out. She ran for the small head within the cargo bay and disappeared inside for less than a minute before returning and getting back in the suit.

"That's twice," Lindy noted.

"Stop counting. It'll save you the stress of being me." The two women ran through their warm-up exercises once more, killing time as they waited.

"Look what we found. An illicit Gate," Clevarious interjected. "I'd like to take the helm. We'll have to go through with the freighter since I have no idea where this one goes."

"Roger. The ship is yours, C. Don't let that ship get away, but we have a tag on it. Even if they were able to slip our tail, we could find them."

"I would like to think so, but stranger things have happened. I'm more concerned that we'll get caught halfway into the Gate when it shuts down. We have to fool the Gate into thinking that *Wyatt Earp* and *Grand Glory* are a single ship. Otherwise, we might get cut in half and relegated to die in the void."

"Don't lose my husband, C," Clodagh pleaded. "What's your plan?"

"I'm placing our prow between the *Glory's* exhaust nozzles. I don't know how our sensors will react, and I'll have to shut down the gravitic shields, or we'll bump them against the freighter, which would alert them to our presence."

Clodagh pursed her lips and unzipped her suit. She climbed out the back and walked slowly toward the head. "Do your best, C."

She didn't have to ask about how the ship would respond to eating the exhaust without shields to protect them. A little extra radioactivity. A lot of heat.

Clodagh used her internal comm chip to relay her next orders. *Everyone get to the back of the ship, secure yourselves in Engineering. Grab Titan and Floyd on your way. Hurry up, people. When we get into position, you will not want to be on the bridge.*

She hurried into and out of the bathroom once more and climbed back into her suit.

Clevarious had already started the countdown. "Eight... seven..." The SI had waited until the last second to get into position to minimize the damage to *Wyatt Earp*. "The Gate is established. In position. Two...one..."

Clodagh held her breath and closed her eyes, even though she was in her suit like Lindy and better protected from a catastrophe than everyone else on board.

Three seconds later, Clevarious reported a successful transit.

"Bringing the shields online. Tracking."

"Where are we?" Clodagh asked.

Aurora replied, "We're in the new system, Tyrosint, but we're angling away from the planet and the station. Looks like we're headed toward another asteroid belt."

"The Bad Company is here. They're not monitoring the Gate?"

"The Gate has been moved and now sits in the moon shadow of the fourth planet. That's why it took me a few seconds to get my bearings."

"Send a coded message by laser to the Bad Company and let them know we're in their system. Make sure they know about that Gate. We could also use backup if they can be ready. They'll need combat suits for a tactical boarding operation if need be. We might be able to convince our bad guys to do the right thing." Clodagh wasn't sure what she could say besides, *Give me my husband, you assholes. Throw in Joseph, Petricia, and Elbinar for good measure.*

She felt bad about being focused on Alant Cole when others were suffering too. It came down on her shoulders like a ton of bricks, and she struggled under the burden until she started sobbing uncontrollably. Her suit was sealed, so no one could see or hear.

Clodagh let it go, wishing for the rush to pass. "Baby brain," they had called it. It came at the most inopportune moments.

"What's the damage to the ship?" Clodagh asked when she could once again speak clearly. She had to blink away the tears, unable to wipe her face or blow her nose.

"Minor, with the exception of the arrays at the front. They've been fried. Clevarious has been trying to compensate by increasing the power to the other nodes. She doesn't know how long it will be before we get a system failure cascade throughout the ship." Aurora sounded concerned.

"All systems?" Clodagh was all ears.

"Only cloaking and shields as they're both tied into the same projection system."

"*Only* cloaking and shields. The good news is that it's a freighter. The bad news is we don't know what's waiting in the asteroid field," Clodagh replied.

"That about sums it up," Aurora confirmed.

Clodagh brought up the main screen's feed to watch the freighter making a lazy approach to the asteroid belt, assuming a parallel course to find where they wanted to enter before diving into the rocks and debris.

Asteroid density in this field was less than most. If they fired railgun projectiles into the area, most would continue out the other side, not having hit anything.

It didn't call for the most precise flying, but the freighter wasn't taking a chance. Clodagh checked the low energy signatures to confirm that Cole, Joseph, and Petricia were still on board.

She sent a message with the latest details to the Magistrate using the Etheric communications system and reinforced her request for Bad Company assistance. There were no inbound messages with their response.

The Magistrate didn't answer, so she left the message with Margaret.

Clodagh dialed the direct link to Lindy. "I feel like my ass is hanging out here."

"I'm sure Cole would tell you that it's a cute ass," Lindy quipped. "It's called faith and confidence. She trusts you. She trusts all of us to do the best we can, and she knows you won't give up on any of them."

"No. I won't. We'll rescue all three, no matter what else happens. If we've followed the right scumbags, then maybe we'll rescue all four."

"I'm ready to go whenever you need me." Lindy climbed out the back of her suit. She scratched her face, head, and body. "That's one big drawback of the suit. It makes me itch."

Clodagh climbed out too. She blew her nose first, then scratched. She stood there for a few heartbeats before heading for the bathroom.

"You have got to be kidding me," Lindy called after her.

"Wait until you find out for yourself before you give me any shit."

Lindy accessed the screen on the side bulkhead that tied into the rest of the ship. She had heard the chief engineer's conversation regarding the external nodes. "How are we doing, C?"

"I don't know how much longer we can maintain an active cloak. I've shut down the shields to limit the flow of energy, but we're at a hundred and fifty-four percent of recommended power flow."

"Engineers always lowball the numbers. We'll be good."

"Not when the engineers are Ankh and Erasmus," the SI replied. She brought up the screen to show the freighter turning ninety degrees to take a line into the asteroid belt. "I'm closing the gap."

Clodagh reappeared and peeked over Lindy's shoulder at the screen to bring herself up to date. "They're going to fail any time now."

"Contact," Clevarious said. "Another ship. A freighter, much bigger, located behind one of the larger objects in the field."

"Can we shut them down with the EMP weapon?"

"Need the nodes," Clevarious replied.

"Suit up," Clodagh said.

"The screening system is failing." A moment later, Clevarious confirmed the pronouncement. "Screens and shields are gone until the nodes can be replaced."

"Prepare to fire the railgun, plasma cannon, and missiles."

"Say what?" Lindy wondered.

"Being prepared to fire isn't the same thing as firing," Clodagh explained. "I'm not going to blow up Cole and the others. We want something left to get our retribution."

Lindy eyed the other woman. "We secure them for the Magistrate. That's what we have to do. We don't have the luxury of taking the law into our own hands. Please,

Clodagh. Don't compromise what you are—what we are—by jumping to the wrong side of the law."

Clodagh hung her head and started to cry. "I'm sorry. You're right. I don't know what's with my head. I want Cole back. I want the team together. I don't know what I want for me, maybe a life not on a ship where we can raise our child in safety."

"This isn't the time..." Lindy started. The freighter accelerated toward the asteroid belt. "Clevarious. Close on our friend but maintain a safe distance. We don't want them to freak out and drive their ship into a big rock. We want them to know they can't escape. That's it."

"Sheepdog," Clodagh said, her eyes clearing. "C, perform some of your magic maneuvers to block the ship. Let it know it has no hope of escaping."

"Gate drive is active," Clevarious reported. "Crossing the event horizon."

Wyatt Earp disappeared from where it trailed *Grand Glory* and reappeared danger-close to the larger freighter within the asteroid belt, blocking the smaller freighter from closing and linking up.

Grand Glory turned one hundred and eighty degrees to throttle up its engines and slow its momentum until it came to a full stop.

"Clevarious, get me the captain of *Grand Glory*, please."

"Not the bigger ship?" Lindy wondered.

Clodagh gripped Lindy's shoulder. "Thank you for helping me focus, think through what needed to be done. The big ship has done nothing to us or against us while we know the smaller ship has three of our people on board. Will this big ship come to their rescue, or will they claim no knowledge? Stay tuned for next week's exciting episode of *As the Asteroid Belt Turns*."

"Where have you been all this time?" Lindy quipped.

"Captain Yuan'gar is on the line, Chief Engineer," Clevarious stated.

"This is Captain Clodagh Cole of the heavy frigate *Wyatt Earp*. You are ordered to heave to and prepare to be boarded. You have three of our people on board, and we want them back. We also want the Furlorians who loaded those three onto your ship."

"I don't know what you're talking about. What's a Furlorian? And you are interfering with my right of free passage. I see you're a Federation vessel. We are not in Federation space. Please move your scow."

Clodagh rolled her eyes. "Magistrate Rivka Anoa and the Bad Company secured this space for the Federation from the pirates occupying it barely a month ago. Consequently, we must assume you're pirates, too, using an illicit Gate. Both your vessels will be seized, possibly temporarily, depending on your level of cooperation."

Clevarious muted the line. "We've deployed a maintenance bot to replace three of the key nodes to attempt an electromagnetic pulse to disable those two ships."

"Good work, C." Clodagh chewed the inside of her lip, waiting for the *Grand Glory* to answer.

"Present yourselves and your credentials at the starboard airlock. Yuan'gar out."

The tactical screen returned.

"Credentials..." Clodagh muttered. "Clevarious, do we have a warrant or anything signed by the Magistrate in conjunction with this case?"

A document popped up on the screen, authorizing the sting and following the kidnappers wherever they lead. "That's pretty broad but good enough for me, C. Shoot it to our pads. Here we go."

Wyatt Earp maneuvered to link up with *Grand Glory*.

"We can't fit through the airlock like this," Lindy pointed at the suits. "Full combat gear?"

"It's just me and you. I'd rather not."

Groenwyn and Lauton appeared. "It's not just you guys. We're here. We volunteer to go with you."

"And me!" Ryleigh called from the corridor.

"And me," Sahved added, looking sad because he had been forgotten.

Lindy took stock of the odd squad. It was a tactical operation at this point, so she took charge.

"All of us, full ballistic protection. Ryleigh, Clodagh, and I will be armed. Sorry, Lauton, Groenwyn, and Sahved, you guys aren't the shooting types, but what I'll need you to do is track the signals from our people. Clodagh and Ryleigh will hold the crew at bay until we get back. Aurora and Kennedy remain aboard *Wyatt Earp*. Secure the damn airlock behind us. Do not let anyone from the freighter board this ship."

They headed into the corridor where the gear lockers held the body armor and suited up: torso protection, legs, arms, and helmets. Ryleigh looked uncomfortable as she checked the hand blaster Lindy gave her. Lindy handed her a stunner as well, tucking a second into her own belt.

"You'll know when to shoot. Don't fire before then. Aim center mass and shoot twice, just like you were taught. All things being equal, no one will die today." She clapped the smaller woman on the shoulder.

Lindy carried two blasters but also took a boarding axe, a gift from Christina and the Bad Company. It had a spike on one side, a rounded blade opposite, and a pry bar on top. She kept one blaster in its holster and carried the other blaster in her right hand and the axe in her left.

The airlocks synced and equalized. Ankh appeared wearing his goggles on his forehead and coveralls.

"I'm going, too," he said.

"It's not safe," Lindy shot back. "You need to put on your armor."

"If they mess with us, I will kill them with my brain." Ankh stared at Lindy as he spoke, unblinking.

"Well, okay." She couldn't think of anything else to say. He came across as deadly serious in his emotionless delivery. "Sahved, you stay with him. Guard Ankh until I tell you differently."

Lindy went through first, with Clodagh behind her, armed primarily with a datapad showing the Magistrate's approval of the operation in which the *Grand Glory* had been caught.

Groenwyn and Lauton followed next with a small scanner that was programmed with the signal from their three people. Ryleigh brought up the rear.

The hatch opened to show three men in filthy clothes carrying stun guns and shot-pistols. Lindy waved those behind her to the side, out of the line of fire.

"Put your weapons on the deck and back the fuck up."

"Nice mouth," one grumbled. It was the voice they'd heard before.

"Captain Yuan'gar, I presume. Put your weapons down, please. We're boarding your ship, and we're getting our people back. Period."

"Is that all you have? A bunch of girls is going to take my ship."

A small body bumped past, and the men looked at him.

"You brought a Skaine?"

Ankh waved at them as if they were inconsequential. "You will seal yourselves inside your cockpit. I've disabled your ship. You will wait there until we're finished with you."

"How do I know you're not going to steal my stuff?" the captain growled, straightening to loom over Ankh. Lindy nudged him backward using the point of her axe.

"You don't, but if we wanted your stuff, you'd already be dead. Go to the cockpit and lock yourselves in. Right now." Ankh stared as they walked away, grumbling and glancing over their shoulders. A hatch slammed and squealed as it was secured.

Lindy stepped through and to the side. "Ankh, you glorious bastard!"

"I don't have parents. No Crenellians do." Ankh looked as confused as he could while wearing a blank expression. He turned and walked aft, pulling his night vision goggles over his eyes.

"That was really fucking weird," Clodagh muttered as she hurried past Lindy to follow Ankh. Groenwyn and Lauton ran to catch up.

"Wait here with me," Lindy told Ryleigh. The younger woman looked relieved and remained in the airlock hatch, peeking left and right down the corridor, hesitant to step onto the freighter.

After the first shot from the blaster, Lindy took off. At the sound of the weapon's rapid fire, she sprinted as if other's lives depended on it.

CHAPTER FOURTEEN

Batik Magal, Delegor

"Tyrosint. I'll be damned. I thought that fucking vampire was holding something back," Rivka said after getting the message from Margaret. They left the cab on the street and used the pedestrian entrance, rushing to the door and walking through since it was open.

A receptionist's head shot up in surprise at the intrusion. Rivka held out her credentials. "I need to talk with someone in charge, and that needs to happen in the next ten seconds, or I'm going to start breaking down doors."

"You can't do that. You aren't allowed in here," the receptionist stammered, standing and holding out her hand as if that would stop the Magistrate.

Rivka took her by the wrist. "Is this clinic involved in blood transfusions using enhanced blood?"

"Enhanced blood?" the woman asked. They received shipments with no questions asked for the wealthiest clients. One was in right now, at the end of the hall.

"Thank you for your cooperation." Rivka slammed her

into her chair and spun it to disorient the woman before she ran through the door and down the hall on her way to the patient room where the ambassador was getting juiced.

She burst through the door, throwing the doctor over his patient. A needle was still in the ambassador's arm, and a bag of blood hung on a hook above the bed.

"What the hell is this?" the doctor demanded.

"I'm arresting you for trafficking in illegal blood. And you, Ambassador! Shame on you. Kidnapping, theft, torture. I'm sure there are a few more crimes of which you're guilty."

The ambassador's mouth pursed into a thin line. "I demand to be tried on Delegor for what you will learn is not a crime. At the end of the day, Magistrate, it will be you who is apologizing and facing jail time, not me."

Rivka avoided touching him so as to not taint her judgment, but she did grab the doctor. "Where did you get this blood?"

"From our normal supplier called Blood Supplies Limited. It's standard practice to rejuvenate old cells with new."

"Chaz, take a look at that blood. Is it enhanced?"

Chaz dabbed gauze at the needle entry point while the blood continued to flow into Ambassador Bik Tia Nor's arm.

He pulled it aside and used the sensors built into his system. He ended by dabbing it on his tongue. Rivka and the doctor recoiled in equal measure while the ambassador chuckled.

"I believe this blood is from Private Elbinar."

"Possession of stolen property that has passed from one

sovereign territory to another. Add that to the charges, Mister Ambassador." She turned to the doctor. "And you, show me everything you have on this Blood Supplies Limited. Who is your contact, when do you get your supplies, how much do you pay? All of it. Tell me all of it. Chaz, accompany the doctor to gather his records. I'm issuing a warrant to search all systems related to acquisition of blood products from Blood Supplies Limited and the distribution of those products. I'll need all those names and addresses."

Chaz ushered the doctor out and hurried him down the hall.

"You think you're bringing a reckoning to Delegor, Magistrate? Do you think you've found what you're looking for?"

"I think that's the last illegal transfusion of stolen enhanced blood you'll ever get. You'll age normally from here on out, maybe quicker since your body has gotten used to repairing itself. It may try to eat itself from the inside out. That wouldn't be optimal, Mister Ambassador. Maybe you'd like to purify your soul and tell me the truth about all this."

"I don't think so. I'll wait for my trial tonight, as per Delegor law."

Rivka stared at him while she stepped back to lean against the wall. The blood bag was almost empty. She removed her datapad and accessed Delegor law. Could she risk pulling the ambassador to the Federation level for trial?

She glanced at him. He watched her, a smug expression on his face. Confidence born of nanocyte-infused blood coursing through his veins. The very crime of which she accused him gave him the strength to defy her.

The ambassador finally removed a small device from his pocket and made a call. "Mads, Bik Tia Nor. Sorry to bother you, but it seems I've been arrested. I'll meet you at the courthouse in about an hour. I'll need to go home and change first. Make that two hours. We'll prepare the case then. Fine. Kids are great. And yours? Getting big. Cold ones on me tonight as soon as we're clear of this farce."

"Farce? Very nice, Mister Ambassador." Rivka tapped her datapad until she found the form she was looking for. She transmitted it to Chaz, who accessed what he needed while downloading the clinic's files. He returned the form filled in as Delegor required. "Your writ of appearance has been transmitted. See you in court."

Rivka left the ambassador behind, reeling from what she'd seen of Delegor law. She needed to wrap her head around their procedures, and she only had four hours to do it. Haste was a priority in trials on Delegor. No one cooled their heels in jail. All criminals were either caught in the act, the crime instantly provable, or they weren't charged.

There was a certain efficiency to it that Rivka appreciated. Did she have enough to prove the ambassador's guilt in crimes as defined by Delegor and not the Federation? That was the question she and Chaz needed to figure out over the next four hours.

She stormed down the hall to where she could see Chaz looming over the doctor. Rivka joined him to find the doctor staring back angrily.

"Your victims are kidnapped and left in comas while

they are continuously drained of their lifeblood. That's what we call the blood trade, and it's illegal as hell. What happened to 'do no harm,' doctor?" Rivka demanded.

"I'm not doing any harm that *I* know of. I'm helping my patients. I buy the blood legally. Where it comes from is not my business, but with your information, I shall no longer do business with them because the provenance of their product is called into question."

"Nice try. If I come back here, you'll be in a world of hurt. Chaz, do we have all the doctor's details?"

"We do, Magistrate."

"Freeze all his accounts, and while you're at it, freeze the ambassador's accounts, too. We may be unlocking them again tonight, but until then, we'll make sure these two stay close. Takes credits to travel. Have a nice day, doctor."

Rivka and Chaz left the clinic. "I'd love to burn this place to the ground. It's what they deserve, but I'll resist." Once outside, she stopped. "But if he doesn't buy from them again, will we have achieved our short-term goal of ending the immediate gratification of the blood trade? Will he be able to resist the high-end clients wanting their fix?"

"What did you see in the ambassador's mind?" Chaz asked.

"I didn't do it. I didn't touch him and didn't look. He's an ambassador. I don't want to be accused of intergalactic espionage. I know he knew where that blood came from, but how do I prove it within the limits of Delegor law?"

"Can't you pull it to the Federation level?"

"Yes and no. We'll do it right here and the ambassador can owe me for not dragging him into a Yollin court, where he'd be found guilty and end up doing time on Jhiordaan, but that probably wouldn't endear us to Delegor. I have those Federation politics to keep in mind. With the rise of the Singularity, they all know who I am." She ground her teeth and clenched her fists. "I hate politics but am left with no choice but to play by their rules. I bet we'll find the same thing with Mastus and Foromme. Let's pull the string on Blood Products Limited, whoever those fuckers are."

They hurried to the street to find their cab was gone.

Grand Glory, Asteroid Belt, Tyrosint System

Clodagh had one hand on Ankh's shoulder, keeping him behind her while she aimed into the darkness beyond. Groenwyn called for calm, and Lauton covered her ears with her hands against the thunder of Clodagh's blaster.

Lindy worked her way through the group to stand beside Clodagh. "What's up? Looking to improve ventilation on this old tub?"

"The Furlorians. They're down there, but they move like smoke in a brisk wind."

Lindy holstered her blaster and removed the stunner from her belt. "Let's see if we can spread the love." She set the stunner for an area engagement, greatly weakening its effect over distance. "Gotta get closer. Please don't shoot me."

She ran forward, closing on the two suspects, a small female clinging to the wall while a larger male hung from the ceiling. Lindy pressed the button to send a muscle-slamming pulse into the space at the end of the corridor, then dove to the side and fired again.

The Furlorians tried to maintain their holds but lost their grip. They both hit the deck, trying to remain upright. They staggered sideways. Lindy stood and hit them again. She closed and fired one more time. Both collapsed under the final engagement. She secured their hands and feet with zip ties in time to find Ankh heading into one of the many cargo sections of the freighter.

Clodagh followed him in. She gasped at what they found.

Lindy wanted to join them and looked at Groenwyn and Lauton for the next task, but that wasn't their job. "Help them," Lindy said, and they went inside. With a grunt, she managed to pick up both her Furlorian bundles and carried them back to the airlock. She dumped them on the deck in front of Ryleigh.

"If they come to, stun them." Lindy hurried aft to find a portion of the cargo bay was set up as a blood collection area. Their friends were unconscious and hooked up to an intricate set of tubes and wires. Ankh was studying the setup but had not yet taken action. A humanoid cowered in the corner. Clodagh tried to watch him while being distracted by having Cole close to being free.

Lindy let Ankh continue his examination as she went to the person who had most likely set up the equipment.

"Name?" Lindy requested.

"I'm the doctor," he managed to squeak.

"You're a fucking criminal, and your road to getting through this without being skinned alive starts now. Unhook these people."

"As I've already told your colleagues, that's not possible. Unhooking them will create a shock to their systems which could very well kill them." He held his hands in front of him as if warding off harsh lights.

"You see, we're not going to buy that because we want our people back and we'll have them." Lindy removed her axe and swung it in a figure eight in front of the doctor, moving closer centimeter by centimeter. "This is going to get extremely painful for you if you don't help us."

He closed his eyes and put his arms across his chest as if surrendering to death. Lindy stopped the intimidation charade and slapped the axe back into its magnetic holder on her back. She grabbed him and dragged him to Cole's side.

"What does this tube do?" she asked, going from one to the next. Ankh paid attention until he nodded. He had a plan.

"We change the inbound nutrition supplements slowly until we're providing the usual IV solution. We reduce the electrical stimulus from running a marathon to sleeping. We eliminate the blood drain first and foremost and let their bodies build strength to manage the changes to the other two processes," Ankh explained. "It's not as difficult as the doctor made it out to be."

"But the shock! They've been on the system long enough—"

Ankh pointed at him without looking.

"The big man said, shut your sewer," Clodagh snarled. "What the fuck else is on this ship?"

Fear grew in the doctor's eyes. Lindy grabbed him and

secured his arms and wrists with more zip ties before he could do anything extreme.

"Your days of doctoring are over," Lindy told him.

"Tell us what you need us to do," Groenwyn offered.

Lindy looked at them and then at Clodagh. "Clodagh, take the doctor to join the Furlorians. We need someone a bit meaner than Ryleigh to watch over them. Can you do that for us? We will make sure Cole is taken care of, but I need you there more than here."

Clodagh touched Cole's leg. It twitched at her touch, and she almost melted. "Okay," she agreed after one last squeeze of his thigh. "Come on." She grabbed the doctor, shoving her arm under his and pulling up until she grabbed his collar. He bent forward under the armbar and stumbled ahead as Clodagh forced him out of the cargo bay and into the corridor.

Groenwyn and Lauton went from patient to patient while Ankh decided on a course of action to bring the three safely to consciousness. He checked the machinery before accessing the programs running it. He slowed the electrical stimulation first.

"Remove the blood taps," Ankh ordered.

Groenwyn grimaced but knew she had no choice. She and Lauton had to do it since there was no one else. She tightened the clamp on the tube to keep the blood from dripping out of the bag.

"For you, our friends," Groenwyn whispered. She removed the bandages holding the catheter, gripped it firmly, and with a tug, pulled it out of Cole's vein. She held the gauze against the puncture for less than a minute before letting up. It had already stopped bleeding, but Cole's pulse was weak.

"Can we turn this around, put his blood back in?" Groenwyn asked.

Ankh blinked up at her. His eyes went blank as he communed with Erasmus. When he focused again on Groenwyn, he had his answer. "That will hasten their return to normal. Let's do it in incremental amounts, a hundred cubic centimeters at a time. Plug the needle you just removed into the feed line of the IV and loosen the clamp, but slowly."

She hung the bag from the same hook as the nutrient feed and added the blood to the drip.

"They could die," Ankh muttered, "if we were complete morons. Vitals are improving."

"The simple act of not taking their blood," Lauton suggested.

"Dial back on the bag. I suspect there are drugs in there to keep them unconscious. We'll add saline from the supply onboard *Wyatt Earp*. Bring them along."

Ankh strolled out of the cargo bay. "What?" Groenwyn asked, looking at the gurney and all the equipment. She waved at Ankh to come back, but he was gone. "How?" She glanced forlornly at Lauton.

"These people are your friends, Groenwyn. We don't have the choice not to do it, so we'll find a way because we have to. Do we have anything to help take the weight?"

Groenwyn left Cole's side while Lauton removed the catheter from Petricia's arm after having already taken care of Joseph. She inserted the needle into the other line before joining Groenwyn to find a way to move the victims.

There was nothing besides the gurneys upon which they rested.

"Looks like the hard way," Lauton said. She piled the attached equipment on the bed, wedging it between Cole's legs to keep it from moving. They released the magnetic locks holding it to the deck and rolled it to the hatch, through it, and down the corridor to the airlock. There they found Lindy, Clodagh, and Ryleigh watching their three prisoners.

"We'll be back with the other two," Groenwyn stated. She and Lauton hurried away, feeling the thrill of triumph. Next, they brought Petricia to the airlock to find Lindy, Ryleigh, and all three prisoners missing.

"They're dumping them in the brig, and then they'll be back to bring our people home," Clodagh explained. "Can you stay here for just a moment? I need to hit the head."

Without waiting for confirmation, Clodagh bolted through the airlock into *Wyatt Earp*.

Groenwyn and Lauton busied themselves by checking on Cole and Petricia and doing what they could to make them comfortable. If they felt anything in their coma-like state.

A noise made Lauton jump. She slapped a hand to her chest, eyes wide at the shape that appeared in the corridor.

Joseph. He continued to pull wires and tubes off his body, tossing them to the deck behind him.

"Joseph!" Groenwyn ran to him, providing her body to help support his.

"You are an angel," he said softly. Groenwyn grunted under the effort to hold the bigger man up. He was dense, like the Magistrate.

"You should still be in bed."

"Nay, lass. I've spent far too much of my life in beds. And this, waking up to being plugged and trussed like a beast, is a nightmare I never expected would be repeated. Who has done such a thing to us?"

"The crew of the freighter is in the cockpit. The Furlorians are in the brig, along with the doctor."

"There were two others beside the Furlorians," Joseph noted.

"Not here, there aren't."

"Drat. We have two escapees on the loose unless they are amongst the members of the crew. The cockpit? This way?" Joseph pointed.

"Yes, but you shouldn't be out of bed," Groenwyn said.

Joseph pushed himself away from her and bounced off the wall as he staggered toward the cockpit.

"Help, somebody!" Groenwyn called through the airlock. "I need help."

The sound of running feet brought her a sigh of relief. First through was Lindy, then Clodagh.

"Joseph is up, and he's headed to the cockpit."

"To do what?" Lindy wondered, working her way past Groenwyn and on board *Grand Glory*. She ran toward the front of the ship in time to get the cockpit hatch slammed in her face and spun closed. "Joseph?"

She couldn't undog the hatch. She settled for putting her ear against the metal and listening. It was quiet beyond. Deathly quiet.

A few moments later, the hatch unsealed and popped open. Joseph walked out, still unsteady on his feet. Lindy looked inside to find the captain and two crew hunched over in their seats. She checked—still alive but in comas.

She caught up with Joseph. "What did you do?"

He fixed her with an icy stare that pierced deep into her soul. "I have dealt with my tormentors. I shall visit the others in the brig, too." He blinked to lighten the negative energy that surrounded him. "It must be done, young lady. They brought it on themselves."

CHAPTER FIFTEEN

Cassiopeia, **Batik Magal, Delegor**

"I don't think I can learn all these procedures in time," Rivka complained. "But you can."

"I already have the entirety of their laws and procedures downloaded and available. I will be able to comply with their guidelines," Chaz replied confidently.

"_We_ will be able to comply. Can two prosecutors ask questions?"

"No. The entirety of Delegor law is based on efficiency. Keep that in mind for all we do. Limited paperwork. One doesn't build a foundation for the suspect's guilt. It is stated and reinforced. That's it."

"This shouldn't take long, then. What kind of punishment is available?"

"Generally a mind infiltration. Hypnosis to cause the guilty pain when they think of issues surrounding that crime. Taking property that's not theirs, for example."

"That would work. The crime is vanity. Standing on other's backs to lift yourself above them, Mister Ambassador. Your punishment is humility. Get your hands dirty. Accept being one of the people, you fucking toad."

"You were so close, too, Magistrate, but alas, none of that is a crime on Delegor. I think the charge of being in possession of stolen property is, how do you say it, a slam dunk? But that's it. Trafficking, kidnapping, none of the big crimes. Possession isn't even a felony here."

"I'm taking the ambassador to trial over a misdemeanor?"

"It would appear so," Chaz remarked. "I've found out what happened to our cab. It was reported as stolen and recovered."

"If we want another cab, will they send it?"

"Probably. I don't think they've linked the broken code to us."

"Did we pay the bill for the travel?" Rivka wondered.

"All of it and then some. We cannot steal what we paid for, Magistrate. I've verified that with the local business charter and laws."

"Then how did it get reported as stolen?" Rivka stood up in the small ship, decided she couldn't pace, and sat down again.

"It wasn't where they thought it would be. I think it should have been logged as a software failure and not as a stolen vehicle. I've registered a complaint with the cab company."

"Good call, Chaz. I'm off my game. I'm worried about everything else that's going on. As a matter of fact, Margaret, get me *Wyatt Earp*, please."

Chaz smiled. "I like how you always say 'please' when talking with one of us."

"Common courtesy, Chaz. Thanks for your help, too. This whole thing with Bik Tia Nor would be a nightmare if I had to learn the nuances of Delegor law. That's about a year's worth of study."

Margaret interrupted. "I have Clevarious for you, Magistrate."

"C. 'Sup?"

"Good news, Magistrate. We have recovered Cole, Petricia, and Joseph. We have the two Furlorians in custody. We believe we know where Private Elbinar is and will continue to pursue that lead."

"Are they okay?"

"Cole and Petricia are still unconscious, but Joseph has come out of it, and, well...you'll have to hear it from the others."

"Then give me someone else. Lindy or Clodagh, please."

"They are busy bringing the injured on board. They are still on gurneys. The crew is limited to its smallest and physically weakest members."

"Lindy isn't weak. What the hell are you going on about, C?"

"Lindy is the exception. The other members are muscling the gurneys through the airlock."

"Give me Clodagh, please."

"One sec," the SI replied.

Chaz maintained a neutral expression.

"Magistrate. It's, like, real work out here, but we have them back. Next stop is this big motherfucker on the other side of us to get Elbinar, but we'll wait for Bad Company backup. It won't be too much longer."

"What did Joseph do?"

Time passed like slowly dripping water before Clodagh answered, "I don't know. When we found them, they were unconscious, almost in a coma."

"They shouldn't have taken him." Rivka wasn't very sympathetic about the retaliation after the violation of his body. "Again. But I'll take a look when I'm back. I won't rush to judgment."

"Something else, too. We rescued our people because of Ankh. He forced the crew of *Grand Glory* to stand down. They thought he was a Skaine."

"But he's not blue. Good for him. Did he say why he did it?"

"Not a word."

"Ted and Joseph are old friends. They've been together for about a hundred and twenty-five years," Rivka explained.

"That's probably it. Ted made a call on Joseph's behalf. Ankh will do anything for Ted."

Rivka opened the hatch on the yacht to get fresh air. "Thanks, Clodagh. If anything changes, let me know, but I'll be in court soon. We caught them giving the ambassador Elbinar's blood. After this short trial, we'll be back in space, hunting down an organization called Blood Supplies Limited. If we have the Gate closed off, then they aren't moving any of the blood currently in stock. We may have already accomplished the primary goal of the case, which was to interdict the blood trade. Once we have Elbinar in hand, we can declare victory. I'll be there as soon as I can. The Gate to Tyrosint is in Fenegus. Send the coordinates to Margaret. We'll be rocking the yacht. Look! There's Tyler. Call if you have anything."

Doctor Toofakre walked slowly. Under the late afternoon sun, he sported a pale shade of green. He stumbled inside.

"What took you so long?" Rivka asked.

"That was the worst food of all time, and I had to down a triple portion of it. I took my bullet for you, Rivka. I'm a member of the club. Now, if you'll excuse me, I'm going to heave my guts out."

Tyler staggered toward the hatch, leaning against it as his stomach rebelled from the abuse. The sickening splatter came moments before the smell filled the cabin. Rivka wrinkled her nose. "Margaret, vent the air. Vents, full power, give me a hundred and ten percent! I'm giving her all she's got, Cap'n."

Chaz sat pleasantly, unaffected by sight, sound, or smell. "I love being me," he told her. Rivka held her shirt over her face, trying to take shallow breaths until the cabin air had been cleansed.

Chaz cleared the one couch, and the doctor reclined on it. Rivka doused a washcloth with water and put it on his forehead. She gave him a bottle of water too, but he didn't drink. He remained where he was, lying there with a rag cooling his head. "It was horrible," he mumbled.

"You took one for the team. We caught the ambassador juicing. We could have used you to explain some of the technical details of the transfusion, but we each have our role to play. They recovered Joseph, Petricia, and Cole. Just one more to drag from the clutches of the scumbags. We're close to gutting this organization. And Chaz, be a hon and clean the puke off the hatch, please."

Tyler's chest rose and fell regularly. "You've caught the ones running it?"

Rivka slouched against the wall. "We've caught the foot soldiers but not the general."

"You've interdicted the trade for a short while, but as long as the leadership remains, they'll establish it anew. The warriors won't be safe anywhere. Supply and demand. As long as the demand exists, someone will step up to supply it. And there's big money involved, which changes the dynamic. My mind is exceptionally clear, but my stomach resents me." Tyler tried to sit up but found it to be too great an effort and flopped back down. Chaz took the pilot's seat, mostly unused since Margaret flew the ship wherever they needed to go.

"At least we'll get our people back, assuming Private Elbinar is on the big ship that *Wyatt Earp* has cornered.

"Is Onyx open yet?"

"They should be. Margaret, get me Team Talon."

"You mean, Red and Dennicron," Margaret sniped back. Rivka made a face and nodded.

"Magistrate. Orders?"

"Can you leave?"

"Yes. The station is now open and in business."

"Bring the *Vengeance* to Delegor and pick us up. We'll depart as soon as this evening's trial is over."

"Why do you have to wait?"

"Efficiency and expediency. The only way to leave earlier would be to drop the charges." She looked at Chaz for confirmation, and he nodded. "I'm not willing to do that. I need to demonstrate that the ambassador is involved in the blood trade and the illegal acquisition and distribution of enhanced blood products."

"We'll be standing by. Margaret, guide us into where you are. I don't think *Cassiopeia* will fit in the cargo bay, so we'll rig an energy tether just like we have from *Wyatt Earp*."

"See you soon, and bring food. What the Delegorites eat is somewhat unpalatable, as we've discovered the hard way. Give Nathan my best."

"On our way, Magistrate," Red confirmed.

After the call ended, Rivka stared at the deck. "I should have thought of that earlier."

Chaz shook his head violently, almost to the point of twisting it off his neck. "Sorry about that," he said as he stopped moving and fixed Rivka with his business look. "We should have brought it up sooner. You don't have to think of all of it, only the important stuff. I suggest you study the elements of cross-examination before the trial. I'll summon a car so we can get there early."

Tyler tried to rise again, managing to get where he could rest his elbows on the table. "I hope that green you've got going isn't permanent," Rivka told him.

"I was going to insist on going, but I think I'll remain here and hold down the fort. Did I hear that Red is bringing real food?"

"He will have something that will settle your stomach. I wonder if your issues are related to new nanos, too. Your first treatment, so your gut is still figuring itself out."

"I'm pretty sure it has everything to do with that horrendous meal I was forced to consume."

"At least your teeth are in good shape for all the chewing." Rivka smiled.

Tyler laid down again and waved his free hand, adjusting his wet rag with the other until it covered his eyes. "Kick the riffraff out, Margaret. I need sleep."

"You heard him," Margaret noted. "Off you go. Win your case. And by then, I expect we'll have *Destiny's Vengeance* looming nearby. Go on, now."

The SI chased the Magistrate and the SCAMP off her ship.

As soon as they were clear, the outer hatch closed.

"Did we just get kicked off our own ship?" Rivka wondered as they stared at the sealed vessel.

Chaz smiled. "How about SIs and their freedom? Go, Singularity!"

Rivka loved the logic train it took for leaving the yacht to Chaz's statement. She clapped at his successful response. Their cab had not yet shown up, so they waited. "What's it going to take to win this case?"

"Have a different case," Chaz said.

"There's a time to be defeatist, and other times when we can't be. I've only lost one case in my life, and that was because I didn't prosecute it well. We haven't prepared as much as I want to for this case, but the usual theatrics have no place in a Delegor court. We had our facts the second we walked in on the ambassador and the doctor."

"Will they hold up to scrutiny?" Chaz asked.

"With no experience in the Delegor court system, I don't know what kind of scrutiny to expect. One would think my word would be good enough, but I doubt that will work. The ambassador's smug expression suggested his word will triumph."

"How about my word? I'm a citizen of the Singularity. My data will stand up to any challenge."

"We'll have to count on that." She nodded at the inbound cab. "Time to put on our game faces. We have a case to try."

Wyatt Earp, Asteroid Belt, Tyrosint System

Two gurneys and Joseph stood in the corridor. The rest of the crew fidgeted uncomfortably. Clodagh meandered until she was face to face with Joseph. "We can't leave them like that. They're incapable of flying their ship."

Joseph shrugged. "Maybe they should have thought of that before they became pirates."

"I think you need to restore their minds."

"I've not taken their minds," Joseph countered.

"But they're brain-dead."

"Not in the least, my dear. They are sampling living through the memories that I've shared with them, memories of what I've done to people. Nothing more. Every day we share our experiences with each other in order to grow as a species."

"Is that what you call growing?" Clodagh pointed through the airlock that was still attached to *Grand Glory*.

"I expect the Bad Company will be able to tow them into a friendly port. With therapy, they'll probably be able to get past the vile nature of their crimes."

"I wish you hadn't done that to them. It's not our place to punish the criminals. It's Rivka's and hers alone."

Joseph nodded. "I submit myself to her judgment. In the meantime, I'll take one of your combat suits and board that big freighter. I'll make sure Private Elbinar is freed."

Clodagh shook her head, not taking her gaze off Joseph's red eyes. "Lindy, secure the suits. No one is to take them or leave the ship."

"Are we going to have a problem, Chief Engineer? Because I don't want any problems. I know what I need to do and what has to be done. No one is better suited to do it than me. The logic is infallible."

"The Magistrate is on her way," Clevarious interjected. "Red and Dennicron will pick them up, and they will Gate directly here. We need only wait a few hours. It will take that much time for the Bad Company to get into position, blocking the freighter. We won't take any action until then. Please, Joseph. Don't go vigilante on us."

"The love of my long life is once again in a coma because there are those who value her blood as a commodity and her body for the blood it provides and not the keen mind and kind soul within. That's twice now. That's *FUCKING TWICE!*" Joseph roared. Clodagh stumbled back until Lindy caught her. "My apologies, lovely lady. Anyone who participates in this blood trade is my mortal enemy. There can be no other way. I'm taking a suit, and I'm boarding that ship."

Clodagh hung her head, her chest heaving, struggling to breathe as she started to sob. A splat sounded as liquid hit the floor.

"Oh, no!" Clodagh cried.

Lindy pointed a finger at Joseph. "I'm with you. Kill them all, but not right now. Everyone put their personal shit aside because it looks like we're delivering a baby, and not one fucking person on this ship knows how."

"I do," Clevarious said. "And you do, too. You were all there for when Vered the Mighty was born."

"Kind of. We didn't do anything," Lindy shot back. "We'll take you to the guest quarters. It's where we deliver babies, isn't it?"

"It's too soon!" Clodagh called, nearly collapsing. Lindy caught her, and Joseph, despite his weakness, picked her up.

"Where to?" he asked, the fire gone from his eyes, replaced by profound sadness. It made Lindy's breath catch.

She shook off the feeling. "Follow me." She walked quickly down the corridor.

"I'll stay with them," Ryleigh said, pointing at the gurneys. Groenwyn and Lauton hurried after the others.

In the small room beyond the captain's suite, nearly across from the brig, Joseph put Clodagh in the bed.

"I could have walked." She grunted under the strain of the contractions, which were increasing in frequency.

"You need to relax."

Groenwyn looked at the door to the brig. "There's a doctor in there," she said softly.

Lindy snarled. "No fucking way."

"Not only no," Clodagh added. "Hell, no and fuck, no."

"We're all going to make it through this," Lindy told them. "Get hot water and towels. Lots of towels."

Lauton took off before anyone else could move. Joseph held Clodagh's hand and moved the hair away from her face. "I'm sorry for causing you such grief," he whispered.

"It wasn't you. I get you. It was that fucker, Cole. Somebody get him in here so I can break his fingers one by one. He said he was an equal partner. Let him feel his fair share!" She started laughing maniacally.

Groenwyn backed away from the door. "Don't you dare," Lindy snapped at her. Groenwyn sulked her way back into the room.

"I was going to see if we could wake Cole."

"Yes, wake Cole!" Clodagh shouted. Groenwyn was off like a shot, leaving Lindy with the business of the baby delivery while Joseph worked to calm the waking dragon.

Lauton returned with a bucket of hot water and four towels. It had to be good enough. "Let's get one under here." Lindy worked it under Clodagh's buttocks and moved her legs into the birthing position. She didn't have to check anything. The top of the baby's head was already visible. Lauton's eyes rolled back in her head and she went over backward, bouncing off the wall and a dresser before ending up on the carpeted deck.

Lindy could do nothing. Her focus was elsewhere. Clodagh had a death grip on Joseph's hand. He was unable to move.

"One more little push. Jumping Jehoshaphat!" Lindy cried as she caught the baby before she shot off the bed and onto the floor. The afterbirth followed, unruptured. Lindy pulled a knife out of her boot, wiped it on her pants, and cleanly sliced the umbilical cord after she clamped it. "Your daughter."

Clodagh held out her arms to take the small but fully formed baby. Lindy tied off the umbilical before wrapping the baby in a dry towel.

Groenwyn returned with a half-conscious Cole leaning heavily on her.

"Alant, isn't she beautiful?"

"I'm sorry to bother you," Clevarious said. "The freighter is moving away."

Lindy looked at Clodagh and then Joseph. Groenwyn couldn't extricate herself from Cole. "I got it," Lindy declared and worked her way out of the room, stopping in the cargo bay to quickly clean up. By the time she reached the bridge, she was still covered in blood, including on her face and in her hair. She didn't sit in the captain's chair because she wasn't sure where else she was a mess.

But her hands were clean.

"Aurora, report."

"We've uncoupled from *Grand Glory* and are in a slow-motion pursuit. They appear to be moving out of the asteroid field."

"Clevarious, get me the Bad Company at Tyrosint."

The comm crackled to signal a connection.

"We're on our way, *Wyatt Earp*. It took us longer to get a ship and crew out of here than we wanted. We were in the middle of a down maintenance cycle when our active ships were called away to deal with a little issue on Tissikinnon Four."

"ETA?"

"Should be at your position in twenty."

"Target is on the move. We'll get him to shut down, one way or another."

"Look for the *Battleship Potemkin*. They'll be there soon."

"Captain Abercrombie. It'll be good to see him again," Lindy replied.

"Sounds like you have it under control. Bad Company out."

Once the line was dead, Lindy muttered, "We have it completely under control. Trust us." She wanted to flop into the chair, but there was still work to be done. "Kennedy, can you plink the maneuvering thrusters on that crate?"

"Say, ten percent charge on the plasma cannon. We can do that. Why just the maneuvering thrusters?"

"A ship without the ability to maneuver through tight spaces will never manage to get through a Gate or even navigate an asteroid field. And the thrusters are some of the easiest systems to fix," Lindy declared. "Aren't they?"

Aurora and Kennedy both shrugged. Clevarious came to their rescue. "The best I can tell you is that they should be."

"Good enough for me. Shut them down but do not blow them up. One of our people is on board. System scan been able to tell us where?"

"There's a dampening field inside that tub," Kennedy grumbled. "We can't see dick."

Lindy snorted. "I see you're learning to speak the language of us knuckle-draggers. You guys should be better than that."

"I learned that one from the Magistrate," Kennedy replied.

"I guess that means I've been overruled. Let's see what you've got. Precise targeting and precision shooting. Commence our combat run."

"A slow-motion run," Aurora said. She maneuvered the

ship away from the freighter's slipstream to move up the starboard side.

"Entering firing solutions. Speed steady at point-five kilometers per second. Passing aft. Fire when we reach amidship. Counting down. Three. Two. One." The plasma cannon snapped off twelve shots in rapid succession. Kennedy beamed at the effort. "Verifying damage. Ten of twelve thrusters are offline. Slow to point one."

"Slowing, aye," Aurora confirmed.

"Retargeting." Kennedy studied the panel. "Targets locked. Firing."

The main switched to show the tactical display. A close-up display of the freighter showed all twelve starboard-side thrusters in red.

Wyatt Earp looped over the top of the freighter, swinging wide to get around an asteroid as the vessel started to fly in a straight line, corkscrewing through space. It tried to rotate to take its port thrusters away from the line of fire, but it lumbered precariously, unable to hold a straight course. Exhaust flares signaled that the ship had throttled up in an attempt to use forward thrust to help it hold a line. During the acceleration, it stopped twisting.

Kennedy locked and fired.

"Six more down. Six to go." The ship held its course. Kennedy fired again. "Two more."

Aurora shook her head. "Moving to a safe distance. Sorry, Ken."

"C, get me the captain of that ship." Lindy moved in front of the captain's chair, standing with her feet spread wide and her fists jammed on her hips.

"They are answering," Clevarious said, surprise in her voice.

"This is…" The ship's captain stopped mid-sentence. "You're beautiful."

Lindy closed her eyes and tried not to be angry. "This is Captain Lindy of the heavy frigate *Wyatt Earp*, on orders of Magistrate Rivka Anoa. Your ship has been implicated in a series of violent crimes. You will move your crew into one section of the ship and then prepare to be boarded."

"Implicated? No. We're a simple exploration vessel looking for the next great haul of rare minerals."

"You are not. You will move your crew to one section of the ship and prepare to be boarded. If any harm comes to the kidnapped person from whom you are extracting blood, you will suffer under the greatest burden of the law."

Joseph strolled onto the bridge. His eyes flashed red and glowed. "I will see pain comes to you, pain from which you will never be free. Imagine being on fire from here to the end of your days."

"Joseph," Lindy whispered over her shoulder, but his focus was on the freighter captain.

"You will heave to, and these good people will board your ship. See that no harm has come to Private Elbinar. That is your only way out." Joseph pointed at the image on the screen. "I'll be waiting for you."

CHAPTER SIXTEEN

Center for Law and Justice, Batik Magal, Delegor

Ostentatious and oversized, the building seemed inappropriate for a system where people would not spend much time within its hallowed halls. Rivka and Chaz registered at the front desk as prosecuting attorneys. They were directed upstairs to the second floor and the courtroom of Judge Dil Abt Nor.

"Is he a relation?" Rivka wondered.

Chaz checked what data sources he could find. "'Nor' is a common first name. Seven percent of the population has it. The last name comes first on Delegor."

"How much don't I know about this place?"

"Without a baseline, it would be problematic to attempt a calculation," Chaz replied.

"Rhetorical question, Chaz. I'm going to show a case of ass in there."

"I thought I was going to ask the questions?"

"You are, but I'll shoot questions to you when I have them."

"I'll do my best, Magistrate." They reached the courtroom, where the door stood open. They were a half-hour early, and no one else was there.

"I guess we make ourselves comfortable until showtime." Rivka strolled back and forth between what she thought was the prosecutor's position and the witness stand.

"That's the spot for the person on trial. Defense and prosecution sit together over here." Chaz pointed at a small area with two chairs and no table.

"I guess I'm in the cheap seats." Rivka looked at the two rows of chairs between the open space and the door to the hallway. She put her coat over a seatback, keeping her datapad in her hand, then pulled up the procedures one more time and tried to race through them. Chaz stood at the prosecution's chair and disappeared into his own mind as he also reviewed the procedures but at the speed of light. He developed the charges that were required at the outset, along with a list of questions that needed to be asked. He left room for the Magistrate to add relevant questions that she wanted asked using the internal comm chip.

At one minute to four, three Delegorites walked in—the doctor, the ambassador, and the defense counsel the ambassador had called "Mads." She didn't acknowledge Chaz's presence as she took her seat. The rest remained standing. Rivka stood as well and waited. At exactly four in the afternoon, the judge walked in and sat down.

He fixed Chaz with a hard stare. "Charges?"

"Possession of stolen property, to wit, the blood of Private Elbinar, misdemeanor first-class case of Bik Tia

Nor. Purchase of stolen property and possession thereof, to wit, the blood of Private Elbinar, felony third-class case of Am Ber Gris."

He remained standing as the others were.

"How do you plead?" the judge asked the accused.

The ambassador spoke first. "To possession of stolen property, guilty of misdemeanor third-class."

Rivka was instantly angry, but there was nothing she could do. Delegor law. Efficiency. No plea deals. It rested at the feet of the judge.

"Where did you get the blood?" the judge asked.

"I bought it from a medical doctor," the ambassador replied.

"Did you know where it came from?"

"No." Bik Tia Nor stood tall as if that answer sufficed.

"Anything else?"

"I am being singled out by Magistrate Rivka Anoa," he pointed as if no one in the room knew she was standing there, "and punished for being who I am, for the very nature of my being. It was inevitable that I would become addicted to the power of young blood, which I was wholly unaware was stolen. I throw myself on the mercy of the court."

"Bik Tia Nor. I find you guilty of possession misdemeanor third-class, which requires no knowledge that the stolen property was stolen. Your fine is five credits. In thirty days, your record will be expunged. The court implores you to seek professional help regarding your addiction."

The judge looked at the doctor, who spoke without further prompting. "To purchase of stolen property, not guilty. To possession of stolen property, guilty in the third class. I did not know the blood was stolen."

"Accused will not add unrequested information. Not guilty of felony purchase. Guilty of possession of stolen property, a misdemeanor in the second class. Your fine is twenty-five credits, and in sixty days, your record will be expunged."

The judge stood and walked out.

The ambassador faced Rivka and snarled, "You'll pay for this, Magistrate."

"Five credits and a clean record. Is that what I'm paying?"

"For following me and invading my privacy on my own planet. You will not be welcome on Delegor. No one here will acknowledge your existence. And I will file a formal complaint with the Federation Council."

"Of course. Make sure you include the part where you were getting a transfusion from one of their people who had been kidnapped. That puts you one step above child molesters. How do you feel about that?"

"Like I've done nothing wrong. A medical treatment for my condition. It helped. I sought more of it. Simple as that. Creating a crime where there is none is deplorable, and you will pay."

"I'm already paying, Mister Ambassador. If you only knew the price of my life! Be on your way. Your case has been adjudicated. And follow the judge's direction. Seek help for your addiction." Rivka glared at him until he stormed off.

The doctor gave her the finger on his way out.

"I think that went well," Chaz said. "My first court drama, and I have emerged victorious!"

"You have an amazing ability to see the silver in a raincloud. Never lose that, Chaz." She slapped him on the shoulder. "Now, let's get the hell out of here. We have our blood trade to tear down, which will deny the ambassador his next fix, and hopefully, everyone everywhere who is counting on this pipeline."

"What if there is more than one pipeline?" Chaz asked.

"Just when I thought you were the silver lining guy, you bring the dark cloud. We'll cross that bridge when we come to it, but for now, I think we're tearing down the operation more than one brick at a time. We're ripping out the entire foundation. It only makes sense they were using a place like Tyrosint. Secured by pirates and outside Federation space."

Once they made it outside, the Magistrate looked for the cab.

"Chaz?"

"It appears that our ability to summon a cab has been restricted."

"They blocked us from calling a cab?" Rivka shook her head. *Margaret, bring the yacht and pick us up. Land in the street in front of the Center for Law and Justice. We can't get a ride.* Destiny's Vengeance *can fly overhead, providing cover if need be.*

Chaz stared into the distance. "Let me try to get the phraseology correct. We shall see if those petty fuckers like the results of their efforts."

"Spot-on, Chaz. Document the denial and prepare the

submission of a formal complaint of mistreatment of a Magistrate to the Federation. Denying us the ability to get a cab. They will inevitably complain about the yacht stopping traffic. Actions have consequences. My dislike for Bik Tia Nor is fermenting with each passing moment. The good news is that I won't have to charge him with obstruction since having Margaret pick us up will be quicker than taking a cab. And my final word is," *Cassiopeia* appeared in the distance, closing rapidly, "fuck that guy and his whole planet."

Chaz didn't bother replying. The yacht swooped low, chased away the light traffic, and landed in the middle of the road. A siren sounded nearby. Rivka strode boldly to the entry hatch, holding her credentials. A law enforcement vehicle arrived. She waved at them and secured the hatch. Margaret was airborne a second later.

Destiny's Vengeance pointed its nose skyward. *Cassiopeia* fell in behind, attaching the energy tether before they bumped through the upper atmosphere and into the beginnings of space. The Gate formed, and both ships slipped through. On the other side, they found an asteroid belt before them.

"Pinging from *Wyatt Earp*. We are three minutes out," Margaret reported.

Tyler sat up and nodded at Chaz and Rivka. She stuffed her credentials into the pocket with the datapad.

"You're looking better," she offered.

"Feeling better. It's amazing what good food can do for one's psyche."

"Good food? I still haven't eaten. Did you snag anything for me?"

Tyler tried to look innocent.

"You didn't."

"I thought we'd be riding in the *Vengeance*. Which begs the question, who'd you piss off now?"

"The more appropriate question is, who didn't I? That answer is 'no one.' I think I've been banned from the whole planet." She pointed at Chaz. "It's his fault."

"What did I do?"

"Let me get in trouble. Shame on you, Chaz."

The SI tried to process the statement.

"Margaret, release the tether and take us to *Wyatt Earp*. Dock in the cargo bay so we can get back to work."

The ship twisted away from *Destiny's Vengeance* and accelerated.

"When you park, you better leave room for at least the front half of the *Vengeance* so Red and Dennicron can join us."

"Of course. I'm always thinking of my fellow spaceships."

Rivka leaned against the bulkhead, trying to think through the case with the ambassador. He was going to make a stink; she felt it in her bones. Deny him his fix. That would be a nice payback. And without the enhanced blood, he would age at an accelerated rate, catching up with where his unenhanced body would have been.

Nothing like explaining to your buddies how you aged thirty years overnight. Fuck you, Rivka repeated. Cassiopeia slowed and bumped to a stop. The hatch popped and dropped, becoming the mini-stairs leading to *Wyatt Earp*'s cargo deck.

Rivka stepped onto the metal and breathed deeply before diving out of the way as *Destiny's Vengeance*'s nose shoved into the space where she'd just been. Red and Dennicron jumped out, and the ship was gone as quickly as it had arrived.

"Don't ever go anywhere without me!" Red bellowed.

"Nice to see you, too."

Dennicron and Chaz hugged in a very human way, then pressed their foreheads together and communed briefly.

Tyler stepped gingerly out of the yacht and headed for the Pod-doc. "Be a peach and spin me up," he asked Rivka. She wanted to go to her quarters and transmit her complaint of and legal action against Ambassador Bik Tia Nor before he could send his trifles. He smiled, but his eyes said he was still in pain.

"More treatments for you. You should be able to choke down shoe leather and be fine," she replied and started pressing buttons on the control panel while he dropped his clothes and worked his way inside the equipment. Once the lid was closed, Rivka pressed start and made sure the Pod-doc was offering the second enhancement to reinforce his previous nanocytes and repairing whatever damage the Delegorite food caused.

"Send me the complaint file!" Rivka called after Chaz.

"Already done, Magistrate."

Giving him the thumbs-up, she ran into her quarters and raised the hologrid. She scanned the file Chaz had put together, added a quick cover letter, and shot it to both General Reynolds and the High Chancellor. She secured the hologrid and went to the bridge.

She found Lindy in the captain's chair, with Red fondling her hair.

"Where's Clodagh?"

"She and her baby are resting."

"Clodagh had her baby? Why am I the last one to find this out?"

"Because you're the last one here. Nothing personal, Magistrate. You were in court, and everything was under control."

"Our ship's doc was with me. Everyone else was… Who delivered the baby?"

Lindy pointed at herself. "Joseph did the handholding and breathing work."

"Well done! We have another dual citizen. Where's Joseph?"

"With Petricia in their quarters. Everyone has come out of their comas. They need to eat and hydrate, and their bodies will heal themselves. We thought about the Pod-doc, but after consulting with Erasmus, it would be of little use."

"What's our next step?" Rivka asked.

"We board that piece of shit and start fucking people up." Red nodded at the ship on the screen, which was moving at a glacial pace through the asteroid field. "Without maneuvering thrusters, he's having a hellacious time trying to get away. What a dumbass. He should have played nice to begin with. Deliver a baby. Blow shit away. The rest of us are superfluous on this ship."

"Just the way we like it, Red. Let me know if Dumbass stops his ship or they clear the asteroids. I'll be with Clodagh and then Joseph. Where are Groenwyn and Lauton?"

"Probably with Clodagh. They feel guilty because they both bailed on me during the bloodfest."

"I'm sure we won't call it that in front of Clodagh. Is Cole there?"

"He made it after the deed was done. Clodagh said he'd never touch her again. During that whole thing, I was having the same thoughts."

Rivka glanced to Red, who looked relieved and then worried. "Hey…"

The Magistrate left the bridge in search of her people. She found a group hanging out in the doorway just beyond her quarters. "Have you been here the whole time?"

"Yeah. We watched you come out talking to yourself and head to the bridge."

"Sometimes I need expert counsel," Rivka replied. She worked her way inside, where the new baby was enjoying fine dining at Chez Mom. Cole was out cold while sitting upright.

"Hey," Rivka called softly. "Congratulations. Are you going to call the baby 'Bad Timing?'"

"It could not have been much worse." Clodagh blinked slowly, barely able to keep her eyes open. "Probably expedited a little bit by the events of the week."

"Three ships scattered across the galaxy, everyone fighting a different battle. And when it came down to it, you were the ones who had to face down the worst of the criminals. Well done, Clodagh, to you and the crew who pulled off the recovery."

"The Furlorians and the doctor are in the brig," Clodagh mumbled. The baby was drifting off.

"Don't worry about anything except your family. You've set the pins up, and it's my responsibility to knock them down."

Rivka rested her hand gently on the baby, whose emotions purred with contentment.

"You're all going to be just fine." Rivka smiled and left the room, stopping when she tried to squeeze past Lauton, who sported a bandage on her head. "What happened to you."

"Baby, blood. Baby down there. Out cold."

"Never seen that before?"

"Zaxxon Major. We're born from artificial wombs in a birthing hospital. There's none of this natural garbage. That looked obscenely painful, and I was not prepared for what I saw and may need bleach to clear it from my eyeballs."

Rivka patted her on the chest. "Life on board this ship doesn't get any better. That's three now born right here in this room."

Lauton shivered from the experience. Rivka let her be and headed for Joseph and Petricia's quarters.

She stopped out front and prepared to knock. The door opened while her knuckles were raised. Joseph stepped into the corridor, closing the door behind him. "Petricia is sleeping."

"Aren't you tired, too?"

"I've slept a lifetime's worth already. I sleep very little nowadays."

"What happened on board the freighter?"

"When one's soul cries out in pain, the fastest way to healing is by sharing that pain."

"You shared it with the *Grand Glory* crew?" Rivka worked to follow what Joseph was saying, measuring it against any crimes he could be accused of, but not by her.

She questioned why she had brought him and Petricia while simultaneously cursing herself for letting them get captured.

"I did. They seemed the most appropriate as their role in bringing my pain was not insubstantial."

"And not the ones who kidnapped you?"

"Their time will come."

Rivka hung her head. "I'm here now. If there's any judging and punishment to be done, it's my responsibility. It's my duty."

Joseph nodded once.

"I can't let you board that ship if you're going to go vigilante on me."

Joseph stared at her.

"I'm sure you can see in my mind that I'm serious. My position is precarious because of the horsepower of those who received the blood. They destroy people with their wealth and power on a daily basis. They don't care about you or me or anyone."

"I won't look into your mind without your permission. I rarely look into others. After four hundred years, I've seen it all, and it remains trying. I prefer not to see others' thoughts. I've seen it on your face, too." Joseph touched her hand, but his emotions and mind remained a void to her.

"Thank goodness I can control it by touch, and people like you and the High Chancellor are blank to me. I'm glad that I haven't seen what you have. I'm torn, Joseph. I want to see everyone associated with this punished to the point that they will never participate again, but the law requires a certain amount of guilt before such extremes in punishment can be delivered. Some of these people aren't fully aware of the crimes they're committing."

"And others are, my dear. I feel for you not being able to judge as harshly as some may deserve, especially those like your ambassador. I think TH might call those like him 'douche canoes,' although I admit that I have no idea what that is. I was raised in a rather different society, and as an adult, my condition set me apart. I am not hip with the youngsters' lingo."

Rivka snort-laughed. "In the harsh climate of where we are and what we're called on to do, a four-hundred-year-old man apologizes for not being hip with the lingo of today's youth. Joseph, you are an exceptional human being. If you can take a look into their minds and point out those in the know, and even more importantly, other links in the chain to help me dismantle this abomination, I'd appreciate it, but you have to promise to leave the punishment to me."

Joseph smiled. "You make a compelling argument, Magistrate. I see why you were called the Queen's Barrister. We must smite those who perpetuate the blood trade. It is too foul to exist. Alas, I shall accede to your wishes for as long as I can to help tear down this monument to avarice. If punishment is called for, I need you to promise that you will deliver it."

"I promise. We will bring Justice to the guilty. We will damn their souls."

"Now you are speaking my language. Whenever you are ready to board, fine lady, let me know." Joseph offered his hand, and Rivka shook it.

He returned to his room, quietly closing the door behind him so as not to disturb Petricia.

Rivka leaned against the bulkhead, collecting her thoughts before returning to the cargo bay to check on Tyler. He was still in the Pod-doc getting his upgrade. She returned to her quarters and blocked the door open. "Clevarious, please ask Chaz and Dennicron to join me."

After a moment, the SI replied, "They are on their way."

Rivka sat on her couch rather than bring up the holo-grid. The series of events leading to this moment weighed on her. She realized she hadn't eaten or slept in two, maybe three days. In space, she lost track of time. She chuckled as she thought about giving Grainger a call and catching him in the middle of his night.

She headed for her food processor to order a sandwich —a triple-stacked bacon, lettuce, and tomato with extra mayo—and coffee.

After the machine dinged, signaling the food was ready, she pulled out her plate to find Chaz and Dennicron standing there.

"There you are," she told them, taking her seat on the couch. The next ding said her coffee was ready. "Be a peach and get that for me, will you?"

The SIs looked at each other, unsure of what needed to be done or why they would want to be a fruit.

Rivka took a big bite, enjoying their confusion as she chewed. Chaz raised his hand.

"Get my coffee for me, please," Rivka clarified, talking with her mouth full.

The lights came on for both Chaz and Dennicron. They smiled at each other and nodded. Chaz secured the Magistrate's coffee. She choked down her current bite and took a drink.

"Have you been able to access anything related to the ship we're following?" Rivka took another bite of her sandwich, feeling better already for having added something to her stomach.

Dennicron took the lead. "We have attempted to access the ship directly, but it is far more than what it appears to be. It has sophisticated systems that prevent scans as well as defeat our efforts at external access to internal computers." She gestured for Chaz to take over.

"We've done a full search for this ship, called LRE-17, which stands for Long Range Explorer. It does not have a name outside this designation. It carries a crew of twenty-four since it is primarily an exploration and research vessel and not a freighter. It is built within the freighter, and that accounts for how it looks. This ship last registered a port of call fourteen months ago, and that was Federation Border Station Nine. It has been out of contact with Federation authorities since then."

Rivka listened quietly.

"Is their lack of ports of call or appearance out here a crime?"

"No," they answered in unison.

"What legal authority do we have to stop them?"

"Known criminals came into the middle of nowhere to seek refuge with them. That is probable cause for a search," Chaz stated.

"Do we know for sure that *Grand Glory* was bound for LRE-17?"

Chaz's and Dennicron's expressions blanked as they accessed their higher computing functions to explore the other ship's databanks, which they had downloaded as standard procedure for any ship involved in the commission of a crime.

The SIs both beamed when they found the answer. "They were most specifically heading to LRE-17, as designated by name from before their departure from Onyx Station."

"Thank you. Next time, let's make sure we have that information before we turn our shlongs into road pizza."

"Shlongs?" Dennicron wondered. "No shlong here, and we don't have to eat."

Rivka shook her head. "Don't try to use that one yourselves. You'll fuck it up. We can't be guessing. It looked like they were heading to LRE-17, but that's circumstantial. It's incumbent upon us to know it for a fact, which we now do. That means I'll drop a search warrant on them, and we'll help ourselves to a look-see. Gin up the rough draft for me, will you?"

Their expressions turned blank as the SIs communed directly. A few seconds later, they reported their progress. "It's in your inbox, Magistrate."

Rivka smiled before finishing her sandwich and returning the plate to the processor for recycling.

She took a sip of her coffee and entered the hologrid.

CHAPTER SEVENTEEN

Wyatt Earp, the Bridge

"*Battleship Potemkin* here, ready to take on the galaxy," Captain Abercrombie said in his best Russian accent.

Ryleigh replied from the captain's chair. "Good to have you here, Captain. We await confirmation that you have taken control of *Grand Glory* and that we have your people on standby, ready to board the freighter known as LRE-17."

"*Grand Glory* will marry up with a tug to tow it to Tyrosint Station in about fifteen mikes. And most importantly, we have a full company of bored warriors, thirteen in combat suits and ready to fly."

"I'll notify the Magistrate. Please standby, *Potemkin*."

Rivka appeared in the doorway before Ryleigh could call her. "Clevarious let me know. Status?"

"They are ready to deploy thirteen mechs as a boarding party."

"Anyone you know over there? Any of you three? I remember our last trip to Tyrosint."

Ryleigh blushed. "Not that you know of," she replied, earning her an eyebrow raise from the Magistrate.

"Do you guys want some liberty on Tyrosint if what we find on this ship wraps up the case?" Rivka had a hostile ship filling her viewscreen, yet she thought about her crew's welfare.

"If we can. It's no big deal if we can't." Aurora and Kennedy made angry faces at their fellow space jockey.

Rivka caught them. "Everyone loves to be the belle of the ball. I'll see what we can do. C, please connect me with the captain of LRE-17." Rivka moved in front of the captain's chair. A snuffle and a snort sounded to her side. She found Floyd bouncing back and forth, looking for attention. She bent to pick her up as the captain came on the screen. Rivka stood, carrying an armload of wombat.

"My. Take a look, Clee. We're besieged by a ship full of beautiful women. When I said this asteroid belt was going to be lucrative, I had no clue how much. Whatcha got there, beautiful? Is that your muff pie?"

Rivka ignored the jibe. "I'm Magistrate Rivka Anoa, and you are implicated in what we call the blood trade. You were going to receive kidnapped persons and stolen property. I've transmitted a search warrant showing our authority and what we are looking for, along with the probable cause justifying the search."

The captain looked off-screen. Another individual called, "It's no good, Captain. Federation people making Federation claims. We don't recognize your authority in this space."

"Let me introduce you to my little friend *Battleship*

Potemkin, who has responsibility for this Federation-claimed territory."

"When did that happen?"

"Less than a month ago."

"We didn't know. You were required to notify us and give us a chance to depart before we become subject to such laws. No, thank you. We'll be on our way."

"Sucks to be you with such a poor knowledge of the law. We call people like you 'barracks lawyers.' They make up something that sounds good. You are a Federation-registered ship in the commission of a Federation crime within Federation space. Do I need to continue? Move your people into a single space. We're coming aboard. If you attempt to flee again, we will disable your ship permanently, and you, captain, will spend the rest of your days regaling your cellmates on Jhiordaan with tall tales of adventure in space."

"You don't have that authority!" the captain shouted at the screen.

"Barracks lawyer speaks. Heave to. We're on our way."

"Listen, girlie, we'll shoot them from the sky if anyone attempts to come aboard."

"Magistrate Rivka Anoa." She held his gaze.

His lips worked and twisted as he prepared a retort.

"Magistrate Rivka Anoa," she repeated. "Say my name."

She drew her finger across her throat, and the comm channel was cut.

"What a pleasant fellow," Rivka said. "Get me Abercrombie, please."

"Why, Magistrate! It's always a pleasure."

"Good to see you, Skipper. Those asswipes are trying to play hardball, so here's what we're going to do. We're going to finish disabling her thrusters, and then we'll ding her main propulsion. She'll be dead in space. We'll tow her out of the asteroid field. The second we're clear, send your people in through both port and aft airlocks. We will be joining you. We have five suits, and we'll use them all."

"You know where the best parties are, Magistrate. See you on the other side." The captain signed off.

Rivka stepped away from the captain's chair. "Ladies. You heard the orders. Disable that ship without hurting Private Elbinar and tow it into open space. We'll be getting our suits on."

"Yes, ma'am!" the enthusiastic trio replied.

Rivka put Floyd down and left the bridge. They had their orders, and Clevarious would make sure their aim was true.

"Red and Lindy!" Rivka bellowed. "Cargo bay. We got ourselves a ship to board. C, let Joseph know."

A cry of "Woohoo" came from close to Engineering, where Red and Lindy's quarters were located. Rivka smiled on her way to the cargo bay. She found Cole lowering the suits from the overhead.

"What the hell are you doing, Cole?"

"Going to fight the Big Bad Wolf, Magistrate. Those fuckers were going to milk me for the rest of my life."

"The ones who took you are in the brig," Rivka replied. "And yes, I believe their intent was to milk you for your blood, and that's why I'm doing everything I can to make sure we resolve this once and for all. We can't have those scumbags preying on the enhanced. There aren't that many of us."

Joseph appeared in the airlock, picked a suit, and walked to it.

"If he's going, I'm going."

"Don't confuse this for a negotiation. I can't have any personal vendettas. Joseph has given me his word. If I let you go, I'll need your promise that you won't start wasting people."

"Even if they deserve it?"

"You can go, but you're not to carry any weapons." Rivka made sure he understood by grabbing him and holding his arms.

"My body is a weapon," Cole countered.

"You can barely stand upright. Don't be a knob."

"I'll come through for you, Magistrate. We'll finish this mission together."

"Case," Rivka corrected.

Red strolled in and cracked his knuckles. He pulled Cole into a one-arm man-hug. "I'm sorry we lost you back there on Onyx. Those slippery fuckers had all the cards. Don't worry, I won't mention that boner thing, and don't you get yourself hurt. Maybe stay behind me and Lindy. For your own health."

Rivka didn't ask.

"Suck my hairy balls!" Cole shot back, trying to push away from Red.

Red pulled him close and whispered, "Stay close to me. If they fuck with us, we'll light 'em up, but listen to the Magistrate. She's the one who says whether it's in the line of duty or murder."

Cole nodded, and Red let go.

The Pod-doc popped.

Cole jumped. "Dammit! Who in the fuck is in there?"

Tyler stepped out and stretched. Lindy turned her back, found her suit, and climbed in.

"Maybe a towel or your clothes," Rivka suggested.

"I feel like a new man!" He flexed and stretched. "Is the floor farther away?"

Rivka picked up his pants and thrust them at him, but they smelled like puke, so she dropped them on the floor. She pulled an emergency blanket from the bulkhead rack and handed it to the doc.

Red shook his head. "You used to be normal, but being on this ship is making you weird." Tyler unfolded the blanket and wrapped it around himself.

"I'm naked, and I don't care," he stated loudly.

"You're naked, and I care." Rivka poked him with one finger. "We're going to board the freighter. Take care of Floyd for us."

Groenwyn walked in carrying the wombat.

"Little girl needs to walk if she wants to be lean like us." Rivka picked a suit that wasn't taken.

Groenwyn put Floyd down. The wombat bounced between people's legs. "I should go with you."

Rivka gestured at the suits. "We're out of gear."

Groenwyn eyed Cole and strolled up to him. "Let *me* go," she said. He tried to brush her off. "You have a tired wife and a new baby. Give them a few minutes of your time. We'll make sure the bad guys get what's coming to them. This is me, and I'm promising that."

She was the one who always looked for the best in people.

"You missed the show. Man Candy was naked and strutting his stuff."

"Red!" Rivka shouted.

"Damn. It's hard to be a man around here," Red grumbled.

"It's hard to be a knucklehead. There's a difference—well, maybe not in your case. What was that about a boner?"

"I take it all back! Jeez. I'm getting into my mech, and we're going to be happy fighting bad guys, my favorite *mission*."

"Who's responsible for him?" Rivka asked. All heads turned toward Lindy.

"Yup. My fault." She raised her hand. "It's hard to be a woman around here."

"Nicely played," Rivka replied, bowing to her bodyguard. She gave the thumbs-up, and everyone climbed into the powered combat suits except Cole. Groenwyn was holding his hands in hers, whispering where the others couldn't hear. He nodded, but his shoulders sagged as he left the cargo bay. Tyler caught up with him on his way out.

Groenwyn took Cole's suit. She sealed herself inside and started running through the operational check.

"Axes," Red said, leaving the oversized railguns behind and settling for breaching equipment instead. Prying something open was far more likely than blasting holes through the bulkheads from a need to kill someone five spaces away. "What kind of loadout is the Bad Company bringing?"

Rivka shrugged, but her suit didn't translate the movement. "No clue. We'll find out soon enough. Open the cargo bay door, please."

"We're going, too," Chaz said from the cargo bay airlock and ran inside with Dennicron close behind.

"Fine. Grab on." Rivka pointed to her suit and to Groenwyn's. The others might be more engaged. Rivka had no intention of getting into a firefight. They had the Bad Company for that.

The energy screen shimmered as the door descended to create a ramp, hanging in space instead of touching the ground to make it easy to get into or out of the bay. Behind them loomed LRE-17, being pulled by the energy tether. *Destiny's Vengeance* flew under her own power on a parallel course.

"Who's flying the *Vengeance*, C?"

"Erasmus himself," Clevarious replied.

"An excellent choice, just in case they try to do something stupid like shoot us down while we're en route," Rivka remarked.

"They better not. That'll piss me off," Red said. He dug out two of the oversized railguns and handed one to Lindy, keeping the other. "Better to have it and not need it."

Rivka wanted to argue, but if the ship started shooting at them while they flew to the airlock, being able to shoot back had some merit.

"We'll wait until we see the Bad Company on their way. We'll follow them in."

Red piped up, "You were worried about Cole going hog-wild on them when thirteen Bad Company warriors are boarding to recover one of their own? I think you should worry more about them."

"You're probably right. C, give me a link to those in their suits ready to head over to LRE-17."

"There you go, Magistrate." The SI was exceedingly efficient.

"Bad Company boarding party. This is Magistrate Rivka Anoa. The rules of engagement for this operation are to avoid firing your weapons if there is no danger. Our role is to find Private Elbinar and anything that might be related to the blood trade. If you find crewmembers destroying anything, stop them. I need the evidence for my case against them."

"We have a few non-lethal systems that we'll test during this operation—net guns, blunt-force projectiles, stunners, stuff like that. We don't usually get the opportunity not to kill people because that's usually our job."

"Roger. Who am I talking with?"

"Platoon Commander Lieutenant Edwin, ma'am."

Rivka searched her mind for where she'd heard of him. "Edwin. You'd been detailed away from the Bad Company for a while. You're special, Pricolici-special."

"That's correct, Magistrate, and quite the memory, considering we've never met."

"I talk to a lot of people and hear a lot of things. Keep your people sharp and try to cause as little damage as possible. That's the big thing I'm looking for. We'll punish the guilty later. That means now we take everyone into custody so we can discuss their life decisions."

"Sounds good, Magistrate. Bridge informs me we're clear of the field."

Clevarious broadcast to all parties. "This is *Wyatt Earp*. We will maintain the tether to ensure LRE-17's position in space remains static. We are full stop, and all systems show green. Good hunting."

"After you," Rivka told Edwin.

CHAPTER EIGHTEEN

Wyatt Earp, **Outside the Asteroid Belt, Tyrosint System**

"Bad Company, play nice. Find Private Elbinar. The focus of our mission is to find him. We secure the ship and its people as we go," Edwin ordered.

Rivka moved to the edge of the cargo bay to watch the Bad Company split into four squads of two, three of which headed over the ship to the starboard side. The final squad with the platoon commander flew toward the port airlock.

"Shall we?" Rivka asked.

Red took a short run and threw himself through the opening, activating the jets to accelerate toward the freighter-looking exploration vessel. As the Bad Company's mechs closed, lasers lashed out from domes surrounding the airlock. The Bad Company blasted outward in a starburst pattern to get away from the fire. Red maintained his direction and raised his railgun. Lindy, by his side, mirrored his aim.

They ensured the firing lane was clear and unleashed on the laser domes. The ship's weapons tried to return fire, but the railguns on full auto were devastating, blasting and scraping the laser transmitters from the hull.

Bad Company swooped back to align on the port airlock.

On the starboard side of the ship, LRE-17 fired more lasers, but the two squads took a different approach, zigzagging to the ship until they were inside the lasers' field of fire. They used brute force to shatter the transmitters, then clumped across the hull until they reached the airlock. Four at a time piled in, weapons hot, and cycled the system.

On the port side, the squad went in first while the platoon commander remained outside.

"A beautiful view, eh, Magistrate?" Edwin said as they waited for the squad to send stun and smoke grenades through the inner hatch after the airlock equalized with the inside of the ship.

The system's star was on the far side of Tyrosint Station, the size of a small moon. The asteroid belt reflected the sun from a light dusting of crystal on the rocky surfaces. Behind them was the ringed giant where the Gate had been hidden. *Wyatt Earp, Destiny's Vengeance, Potemkin,* and LRE-17 loomed in a starship standoff. The battleship's gross tonnage exceeded that of the other ships combined. The exploratory vessel had been ill-advised to be belligerent.

Sometimes criminals were smart, and the rest of the time, they were like this crowd, which confirmed Rivka's suspicions. These weren't the blood trade masterminds, but somewhere on board that ship was information that might lead her to them.

"Don't damage any of the comphuter systems, people. That's what we need to tear these assholes new assholes."

"Profound," Red muttered.

"I'm still tired and hungry. Never go on a culinary vacation to Delegor."

"First Squad is through. Securing the corridor fore and aft. Light resistance has been neutralized," the squad leader reported.

"After you." Edwin gestured toward the Magistrate.

She shook her head. "I'm last. Red, Lindy, Joseph, Chaz, and Dennicron. You'll all fit with the good lieutenant."

It was a tight squeeze, but no one complained. Once they were inside, First Squad moved out, heading aft while Second and Third Squads on the starboard side moved forward. Red and Lindy set up a blocking position at the airlock. Chaz and Dennicron joined Joseph as he went toward the interior of the ship down a transverse passageway that barely allowed a single mech through.

Rivka and Groenwyn stepped into the corridor and tried to get their bearings. The ship's air handling system had already cleared the smoke. Scorch marks on the deck and bulkheads showed where the grenades had discharged.

"Joseph, do you sense anything?" Rivka asked.

He didn't answer right away. "Chaz? Dennicron?"

Chaz replied. *There is a commotion ahead, but Joseph is blocking the way. This corridor is fairly narrow. It might be better to maneuver without the suits.*

But if they're putting up a fight, we're better off in our armor.

Good thing you brought us along. As soon as we can get to a terminal, Ankh and Erasmus are standing by.

Onward, trusty trainees. Break through that firewall, Rivka encouraged.

"Which way, Magistrate?" Red asked. The platoon commander had gone aft, following his squad.

"Forward? Seems to be the only way left."

"Left? That takes us back into space," Red deadpanned. He hatcheted an arm toward the ship's bow. "And then there's more down than up. I think we're on the second of five decks."

"Let's clear this one and move down," Rivka decided.

"HUD shows the Bad Company's Third Squad has already gone to the top deck," Red reported. Rivka checked her settings to find she didn't have the Bad Company selected. She added that, and the HUD populated. The thirteen mechs were moving quickly through the ship. She added heat sources, and that showed bodies in nooks and crannies at various locations.

She watched while maintaining an easy pace behind Red. The warm bodies fell and were wrapped up and passed to the rear, where they were moved to a room behind them. One warrior stayed there to keep them secured beyond the zip ties binding their hands and feet. Eight of the twenty-four crew had already been put out of commission.

Once inside the ship, the sensors worked. Rivka conducted a quick scan to find warm horizontal bodies. "Lieutenant," she started, "are you seeing the people on gurneys two levels beneath us? There are eight of them. That makes thirty-two total onboard."

"We were expecting one," Edwin replied. "This comes as a surprise, but good catch. Second Squad, abandon the first deck and head down to the fourth deck. Secure the personnel on gurneys ASAP."

"Joseph?" Rivka asked, calling her team to a halt. "We're heading down to see what that looks like before the crime scene can be too damaged."

After a moment, Rivka dialed up the Bad Company. "Make sure you record the video feeds from the first warriors to see the space. Give me the best view for court records."

Groenwyn jumped into the conversation. "We've learned how best to unhook them from the system, so if you find they are being drained, leave them to us so we don't accidentally kill any of them."

They had to assume there were more enhanced being drained than just Private Elbinar.

Rivka found that disconcerting.

"Joseph? Where the hell are you? Chaz, Dennicron?"

"We are in a small space with the core computing assets. You want us here. Joseph has moved on."

"Bad Company, please keep your eyes out for Joseph. His suit has been static for two minutes. I fear he's parked it and gotten out."

"Roger," Edwin replied.

"Can't we track him?" Rivka asked her team.

"No. These suits don't have Etheric tracking in them. We have it on *Wyatt Earp*, except that the dampening field is still in effect and they can't see through the hull," Dennicron replied. "We're working on bringing the field down, but this system is stalwart, an SI-produced system but heavily modified. We don't sense an SI on board, which means there won't be active interference, and you know what they say about static defenses."

"A monument to man's stupidity," Rivka replied.

"Exactly that. We'll report when we've made progress. We expect we'll be able to download the core in short order."

Before Dennicron could sign off, Rivka added guidance. "Look for buyers. Look for logistics to get the blood to buyers. Look for someone in charge. That's who I want to talk to."

"Orders, Magistrate? Do we look for Joseph, help secure the crew, or go after the victims?"

Rivka groaned. "We better get below. Groenwyn says we know how to recover the victims. Let's do that. The crew isn't going anywhere."

"But if Joseph gets to them first?" Red wondered.

"I have his promise. It'll be okay. There should be a freight lift."

"Aft," Red said, highlighting the point on the HUDs.

They turned around and Rivka led the way until Red managed to get past her, giving her a hard look through the mirrored screen of his face shield, one that she didn't have to see to know.

Red moved quickly, using the suit's systems to look for threats versus checking each space as they passed, even though First Squad had already been through there. He was focused on getting to the freight elevator, a place the warriors in front of them were beyond.

With a delicate touch, he summoned the elevator and waited.

When it arrived, Red put Rivka and Groenwyn in the

back so he and Lindy could be the first ones into the uncleared area two decks below.

"Lindy goes left. I'll go right. It's only forty meters down the corridor. Third Squad will approach from the starboard side. I have positive contact with the Bad Company, and we are on their displays," Red confirmed.

He took a more cautious approach, moving toward the bay ahead, stopping at each doorway to check even though his systems showed the spaces beyond were clear. Red trusted his eyes and his feelings.

Rivka waited impatiently, but Red wouldn't be rushed. "What's the holdup, big guy?"

"I have a bad feeling about this." He continued his methodical movement forward.

"People are getting vampired right up there. Of course it's giving you the willies. Those people are counting on us." Rivka stepped closer to Red. He opened a door and was inundated by slug fire from within. Rivka stumbled back into Groenwyn. Lindy closed the distance while watching their rear.

Red bellowed at the enemy while rotating his railgun forward and firing into the space.

Rivka winced at the blasts. Her suit attenuated the sound to keep it from damaging her ears, but that was not what worried her. She didn't want the railgun to puncture the hull on the far side of the ship. Red ducked through the doorway and stepped inside. He fired once more.

"Security bots," he reported. "But anti-personnel. The operators of this ship didn't plan on a mech assault."

"It also begs the question of why would a research vessel have security bots down here and not where they would be able to leave the ship." Rivka peeked through the doorway.

"Storage?" Groenwyn asked.

"Then they wouldn't have been active, but they could have activated them once they realized we were coming," Red answered. "This was set up as an ambush. Attack into the middle of a group coming down the corridor."

Weapons fire came from the far corridor.

Rivka checked her HUD and leaned away from the sounds, even though intellectually she knew the warriors only carried non-lethal weapons. "Another ambush?" she murmured.

Red quickly continued down the corridor since there were no more doors except the one to the bay where the horizontal bodies were located. But only six now. Two were up and moving around.

"Stay frosty; we got two walkers. Maybe this is sleeping quarters or a holding cell of some sort," Red suggested. He looked back at the team before doing a three, two, one countdown with the fingers of his mech suit. On one, he opened the door and went through, stopping one step inside the door and sweeping quickly from left to right to make sure his video recorded all the details.

He activated his external speaker and turned up the volume. "Stop what you're doing and get on your face."

Rivka tried to see past him but only caught glimpses of bodies on medical beds, one arm with an IV of clear liquid and the other arm feeding blood into a tube. Electrodes trailed from the individuals to equipment by their heads.

Red stormed into the room. He swung his metal arm in an uppercut that sent a white-robed individual to the far side of the bay to hit the wall and slide down it to crumple on the floor. "I said, stop," he growled.

He moved to the side, seized a second individual, and lifted her into the air. She struggled futilely against the grip. Rivka walked into the bay.

Six bodies were hooked up. She moved as best she could around the outside since the medical equipment took up a great deal of space and the mechs were bulky. Rivka finally gave up, parked her suit, and climbed out the back. Groenwyn followed her lead.

CHAPTER NINETEEN

LRE-17, Medical Bay, Level 4

"We have Elbinar," Rivka announced when she got close enough and was able to lift the mask off his face.

A cheer sounded from beyond the bay. The Bad Company had used the speakers on their suits. They entered slowly so as not to disturb what Rivka and her team were doing.

"Groenwyn, what do we need to do to bring him back to the land of the living?"

The young woman tucked her now-signature platinum-green hair behind her ears and studied the setup.

"This is identical to what we found on the *Grand Glory*. Here's what we need to do..." She described the process step by step as Ankh had laid it out, but the available blood was almost non-existent.

"I guess we give him what we have. It's better than nothing."

"Step one, remove the blood catheter. Replace the drugged bag with a Ringer's Lactate solution. Plug the blood bag into the feed line," Groenwyn recited as she worked on the individual next to the private. Rivka mirrored her movements, removing the blood catheter and putting pressure on the wound.

Red shook the individual he was holding. A female humanoid, similar to a human but without ears. "Where's the Ringer's solution without the coma drugs?"

She pointed at a cabinet. Groenwyn hurried over while Lindy blocked the doorway with her mech and climbed out to provide a helping hand. Inside the cabinet, they found Federation-approved bags of the electrolyte-balancing fluid to aid patients with low blood volume.

"That's not going to mess with them, is it?" Red demanded. She shook her head. Rivka decided they needed a definitive answer. She joined them and grabbed the woman by her wrist.

"Tell me, how do we keep these people alive?" Rivka went a different direction from Red's question in order to make her correct herself.

The first thing she thought of was removing the blood draw, then she worried about the machine. She had been hired to do a job. All she wanted was to leave, and now this...

"Put her down, Red."

Red hesitated but lowered the female to the floor and released her. He hovered in case she had a change of mind but expected the Magistrate saw that she was no threat. Still, he had a job to do, and the Magistrate continued to find new and exciting ways to make it hard.

"Help us save these people." Rivka directed the nurse to a bed. "This is Private Elbinar. He's a member of the Bad

Company, kidnapped from Federation Base Station Eleven nearly a month ago. I don't know who these other people are, but I expect they have similar stories. We need them back in the real world and not as blood factories. Help us to release them. You were thinking about the machine. What do we need to do to transition from donating blood to recovering?"

The female nodded, moved to the head of Elbinar's bed, and started tapping buttons. Rivka tried to follow, but it was too quick.

"Slow down," Rivka requested while resting her hand on the female's back. No subterfuge. A desire to help. "I'm a Magistrate. Your assistance here and saving these people's lives will ensure you leave this place unscathed. I can't promise you that you'll get paid or whatever you're due, but I can tell you that you will not be charged with a crime, while the rest of the people on this ship probably will be."

"I understand," she said. "I'm just a nurse hired to help on an exploration ship. That's not what this is at all. The only thing we explore is places to hide."

"That's the kind of information that will solidify my case against them. Get Elbinar turned around, and all these others, too."

"The Ringer's Lactate." She gestured for Groenwyn to hand it over. She put it on the hook where the other bag had been, now in a trash can nearby. She plugged the new bag into the catheter while adding the blood into the line so they dripped together. She mashed a few more buttons on the machine and moved to the next patient.

Between Lindy, Groenwyn, and the nurse, they quickly had things under control. Third Squad arrived but left when they realized they weren't needed. They still had the crew and ship to secure.

Rivka made to leave but couldn't get around Lindy's suit.

"Where do you think you're going?" Red asked.

"To find Joseph."

"In a suit, crazy woman." Red hammered a metal fist into an oversized metal hand to emphasize his point. Then he pointed at Rivka's armor.

"No, crazy man. I can move faster and get into areas where the suit won't fit. Joseph isn't wearing his, and I need to face him *mano a mano*."

He parked his suit to the side and climbed out, then checked his hand blaster. Rivka showed him the neutron pulse weapon she carried, but the look on her face said she didn't intend to use it.

"On the crew of this ship, but not Joseph. We don't hurt Joseph."

"You have my word, Magistrate," Red promised. He nodded at the door on the opposite side where the Bad Company had entered. "Lindy, let 'em know that we're on the move without suits and not to shoot us."

She nodded tightly, stopped where she was, and ran across the bay to hop into her suit and make the report.

Red led the way, looking for the staircase up that he thought was aft a short way, opposite the freight elevator.

The lieutenant said to get your asses back into your suits in case the crew blows the ship.

Fair point. Tell him not to be disappointed that we're not going to follow his advice, Rivka replied.

I already told him that and encouraged him to do his best to keep the crew from blowing up the ship.

That's my girl, Red remarked.

Magistrate? We are into the system, Dennicron reported.

Make sure the crew can't destroy stuff, including the ship, Rivka ordered.

They wouldn't be able to do that since the engines are offline. I've taken down the dampening field, and Clevarious is now scanning the ship.

Can you tell us where Joseph is?

One level up from you, almost directly over your head. He's with a group of four crewmembers.

On our way. Rivka didn't thank the SIs for their help. She knew they'd be busy digging deep into the core to look for information to support her case and the one who was running the operation.

They hit the stairs at a trot and took them two at a time going up. They left the stairwell, took a hard left, and ran to the first door.

It stood open. Red nearly tackled the Magistrate to keep her from barreling headlong into the space. Red peeked inside to find Joseph speaking to a sedate group.

"Magistrate, just walk in," Red told her but kept Rivka behind him. After he cleared the doorway, she walked around him into the room.

"Joseph," she said.

"Rivka. I'm glad you made it. Did you find the others?"

"Yes, Elbinar is safe. There were five others too, but you knew that."

"I knew it because they knew it. They know a few other

things too, but not everything. Did your AIs get into the computer system?"

"The SIs, yes. They are in there now." She studied the four crew in the room. They stood with heads bowed, deferring to Joseph.

"This one is the captain of this vessel. He knows the most." Joseph motioned with his chin.

Rivka touched his arm and recoiled from the horror surging through the man's mind.

"I asked you not to do anything."

"I did nothing. These men were here. Their minds drew me, but they were already lost, having descended into darkness at the thought of getting captured but too cowardly to take their own lives."

"Then how do you know what's in their minds? I could only see the agony of the evil that they submitted to."

"I am a telepath. I can go as deep as I need. You see emotions and surface thoughts. I need ask no questions to find my answers."

"Red, zip ties."

Red produced their favorite suspect-binding devices. The men didn't resist while Red tightened the temporary cuffs around their wrists.

"Their main contact is from a planet called Foromme. Her name is Koranta Delaveen. She is running this show."

Rivka pushed her fingers through her hair and blew out her breath. The ambassador from Foromme's name was Delaveen. *Clevarious, check if Ambassador Delaveen is related to Koranta Delaveen.*

"Who are those other five people?"

Joseph frowned. "People who had received nanocytes

once upon a time. Their blood is better than nothing but is as potent as water compared to the whiskey of Elbinar's nanos. Those five are volunteers, down and out, looking for a way to make money while buying time away from creditors and their fellows at the bottom of life's cesspool."

"They're here on purpose?"

"They are, my lady," Joseph replied. He looked down, and his shoulders slumped. "I'm tired."

She pulled him into a hug. "I know, Joseph. Seeing the worst that people can do to each other for selfish reasons is enough to rip parts of our souls away. I wish life were different, but it's not. As long as we still have the energy, we need to protect those who can't protect themselves. Let's get out of here."

She supported Joseph as they walked out of the space, leaving the four to their tortured thoughts. Red waved his hand in front of their faces, but they didn't respond. "Fuck you," he told them and joined Rivka and Joseph as they slowly walked toward the stairwell.

Let Edwin know that we're clearing the ship. We have what we need. Elbinar is in good hands. Dennicron, did you get the complete database downloaded?

We did, Magistrate. Meet you at the airlock.

Indeed. Lindy and Groenwyn, meet us at the airlock. Speed is of the essence if we're to cut the head off this snake.

Dennicron and Chaz met them on the third level to take Joseph the rest of the way. Red and Rivka descended to the fourth level to get their suits. The "donors" were already waking up, although their eyes were sunken and their expressions vacant.

"Elbinar, what do you remember?" Rivka asked while touching his arm.

A hot Furlorian. So hot. Sparks. Yeah, baby... That was it. Rivka shook her head.

"You've been kidnapped, and this delightful group here has been stealing and selling your blood. We found a sample in Ambassador Bik Tia Nor's blood on Delegor."

"Delegor? Never heard of her."

Rivka felt her anguish lessen at the private's innocent smile. "Most people haven't, but never fear. You won't be getting that back, but you'll make new stuff. Most importantly, keep it inside your body if you wouldn't mind?"

"I'll do my best, ma'am. Who are you?"

"Magistrate Rivka Anoa. We met on the *War Axe*, I'm sure."

"Are you married?" he asked with a half-smile, his skin still gray since his body was about a quart low.

"I'm flattered. But I am..."

Red and Lindy leaned close. Groenwyn smiled and cocked her head so she wouldn't miss a word.

"I'm seeing someone."

"For fuck's sake," Red blurted and waved a dismissive hand at Rivka. "I'm getting in my suit because shit's getting deep in here."

Rivka ignored him and moved to the next patient, who looked like he was ready to cry. "What's the problem? You're going to be free."

"What about my contract? I was promised ten years and the pay to go with it, fifty thousand a year. What year is it?"

"It is the year twenty-two sixty-two Earth standard,

adopted by Yoll and the Empire nearly one hundred fifty years ago."

"I'm nine and a half years early. I can't go back now! Plug me in."

"This is an illegal operation," Rivka said.

"I had a contract." He started to flail in panic. "No. Plug me back in."

Rivka pushed him down. He was too weak to put up a fight. "For the moment, the Bad Company will take you into protective custody. All of you." Rivka waved her arm around the room and looked at Red.

"Fine, I'll relay your request," Red said using his suit's external speakers.

Groenwyn went from bed to bed, whispering something to each that instantly calmed them. She smiled and touched their faces as she went. At the end, she waved to them before climbing into her suit. Lindy waited until the Magistrate loaded up, but she wasn't ready quite yet.

She returned to Elbinar. "I have the Furlorians in my brig, a brother and sister. I can leave them in the brig on Tyrosint Station if you'd like to see her."

"Would you? That would be great. I think we had something." The man's smile lit the room.

Rivka chuckled. "All she needs is a partner to show her what's important in life."

She's a snake, Red clarified. *Just ask Cole.*

CHAPTER TWENTY

Wyatt Earp, **Cargo Bay**

The five flew into the cargo bay, touching down slowly so the SIs hanging off Red and Lindy could step gently to the deck. Chaz and Dennicron hurried away with LRE-17's complete database in their possession.

"C, set course for Tyrosint Station, best possible speed. We're going to deposit our three prisoners in their brig for future processing. I guess I should deal with them now so I don't have their disposition pending. Maybe Delegor had something going for them with the expeditious nature of their judicial code. Dennicron, Red, Joseph, Petricia, and Cole, meet me in the conference room, and let's see what we have."

Rivka strolled out to find Tyler waiting for her in the corridor. He carried Floyd.

"Look at my beefy supremeness," Rivka quipped, leaning over the wombat for a kiss.

The doctor's face turned solemn. "Do they need medical help over there?"

"I don't think so." Rivka hadn't asked. "C," she called to the overhead, "get me Lieutenant Edwin."

"Magistrate, you miss me already," the warrior joked. "Ship is secure, twenty-four are in cold storage, one casualty in the medical bay, and six coming out of their bloodless stupor."

"Casualty?" Rivka wondered.

"We found him after you guys left. Looks like someone in a suit pummeled him."

"That guy. Yeah. That was us. Do you need any additional medical assistance? We have a doctor on board *Wyatt Earp*."

"It wouldn't hurt. We have the nurse that you left for us. She's cooperating, but she was part of that crew."

"C, new orders. Dock us with LRE-17 so Doctor Toofakre can review the patients, and where's Sahved? I haven't seen him in a dog's age."

Clevarious replied. "He is still guarding Ankh, the last order he received from Lindy."

"Tell him he's an investigator again and get his ass to the airlock to collect statements from the victims in the med bay. We need more information."

"Docking with the freighter, roger," the SI confirmed, spooling down the Gate drive since they were mere seconds from going through and reappearing at Tyrosint Station.

"Thank you. Patients first. We'll catch our bad guys soon enough," Rivka allowed. Tyler stuffed Floyd into her arms.

Whee! the wombat cheered. Tyler went for his gear, and Rivka retired to the conference room to get statements before judging the three prisoners currently stashed in the ship's small brig.

Rivka stroked Floyd's fur.

Hungry, the little girl cried.

"I'm sure you are, but we have to wait a little bit before we can eat. We've got this thing to do."

Groenwyn!

"Let's not bother her."

"You called, Mistress Fluffy Butt?" Groenwyn spoke through the conference room's open door.

Hungry, Floyd repeated.

"Do you want to go back to LRE-17 with Tyler and check on the patients? I would appreciate your gentle touch to help them past the trauma."

Groenwyn nodded but still took Floyd from Rivka's arms.

"Make her walk to get food. If we carry her to meals, she'll outgrow her ability to stay on this ship because she won't fit through the corridors."

Boo. Floyd made a face as Groenwyn put her down. She scampered in the direction of the galley.

"I'll get Floyd a few leaves of lettuce and then meet Tyler in the cargo bay."

"Airlock. We're linking up. No need to jump across the void."

"Better," Groenwyn agreed.

Red and Lindy appeared. "I'd like one of you guys to go with Tyler and Groenwyn onboard LRE-17 to make sure the patients are stable for recovery. But first, I'll need statements about our captives."

Red spoke. "That Furlorian female is the one I saw

leading Cole away. And then Cole was gone, and so was she."

"I like the short and fact-based version. You didn't see anything else?"

"After they got in front of us, a smoke bomb dropped behind them, blocking our view. Coincidence? I think not, but you're the judge. That's your department."

"Cole. Thanks for joining us. How's your little baby?"

"She's cute as a button," Cole said in a tired voice. He hadn't recovered from his bloodletting, and he had not gotten used to sleeping in less than two-hour chunks.

"Name?"

"We don't have one yet. Still thinking."

"Leave it to Cole to put off 'til tomorrow something that should have been done yesterday."

"Kiss my ass, you oversized, under-brained, bow-legged, big-necked, no-load!"

Red snapped his eyes to Lindy. She shook her head. He looked back at Cole. "I don't know if I'm supposed to be insulted or impressed, but I'll take the latter. You can come through in the clutch. What are you going to call number three?"

"Number three?"

"That's the number on her Singularity passport. You got yourself a dual citizen right there. Number one is, of course, and I say this in all humility, Vered the Mighty."

"'In all humility,'" Cole repeated. "Alana. Clodagh is thinking it over. You know, my name is Alant, but all you weirdos just call me Cole."

"Even Clodagh calls you Cole!" Red blurted.

"Still," the man countered before pointing aft where the

brig was located. "The Furlorian. She's smooth and had one purpose: get me to where the others could zap me with a stunner. I was ready for it and they still hit me with increasingly powerful charges, but I remembered the first four."

Rivka stared at the table as she processed Cole's report. "Elbinar didn't see any of it coming. He was smitten by the little vixen. You said she had one purpose. How did you know that?"

He looked around to make sure Clodagh wasn't nearby. "The first night, a nice admin specialist wanted a piece of this." He stood back and modeled his physique. Red made gagging noises before kissing Lindy goodbye as she headed off to join Tyler and Groenwyn. "But the Furlorian, she was singularly focused on me leaving with her based on a promise of bliss. She didn't want to talk or hang out. Maybe she learned that she didn't need to invest that time to get her target into a vulnerable position."

Rivka nodded. "Anything else?"

He shook his head.

"Go back to being a parent now. Alana sounds like a great name. Good luck bringing your better half on board with it. Red, do you want to bring the Furlorians? Do you need backup?"

"I could use someone with a stunner, although I'm going to hit them with an area stun before I step into the brig to retrieve them."

"Take Chaz and Dennicron. If anyone is faster than the Furlorians, it's you three."

"I'm not bow-legged," Red noted.

"Please don't take this the wrong way, but why in the

fuck did you ever think I would care about that?" Rivka dismissed him with a wave and started tapping her datapad.

A short while later, scrabbling and scratching signaled that the Furlorians were on their way. Red had both of them by the scruffs of their necks while Chaz and Denni-cron followed closely, slapping at limbs that sought purchase to drag Red anywhere but the conference room. Once inside, they closed the door behind them. Red continued to hold their prisoners.

"I'd put them down, but they'll start climbing the walls or hide under the table. I'd rather not have to catch them again."

"I'm Magistrate Rivka Anoa. I'm here to judge your crimes and deliver the punishment."

"We've done nothing wrong."

"This is more than just a difference of opinion. While on Federation property, you have to comply with Federa-tion law. That means you don't get to take someone against their will and put them into a coma while you steal their blood. That's the series of crimes that you'll be judged for."

"We didn't take anyone's blood," the female countered.

"Maybe not, but you delivered Private Cole to a ship in space where such things were happening. Even if you didn't know when you kidnapped him, once you became aware and did nothing to stop it, you became complicit in the related crime. I am not only going to charge you and convict you of kidnapping Elbinar, Cole, Petricia, and Joseph, I am also going to charge you with theft, trans-portation of stolen goods, and destruction of government property, specifically the lights and systems onboard Station Eleven."

"Destruction of government property? That wasn't us."

"I believe you. The security contractor was a plant. It was them. You're not guilty of destruction, but I find you guilty of all other charges and specifications."

"Wait! We didn't steal anything either."

"Once their blood was taken and sold, it became stolen property, and you are complicit in the sequential crime. But you may argue that one can only be punished once for a single act even though that act broke numerous laws, and you would be correct. However, the theft and sale of the blood is a separate crime, distinct in its merits and unique in the opportunity for sentencing. I can also charge you with crimes against sentience, which carries a penalty up to and including death."

"Wait!" the male Furlorian cried. "I didn't do any of it. It was her. I wasn't even there."

"We have eyewitnesses who saw both of you and two others load Private Elbinar into a ship."

"You couldn't have seen me!" the male blurted.

"How would you know that?" Rivka asked.

"Shut up, asshole," the female said.

"You don't need to say anything. You're guilty. Both of you. Twenty years each, sentences to be served consecutively, which means you are going to be confined on Jhiordaan for the rest of your natural days. I'm not going to give you the opportunity to say anything because I don't care what you have to say unless you're willing to roll over on whoever was paying you. I can cut your sentence in half with good information that unravels the rest of the blood trade organization."

"And serve all sentences concurrently," the female said.

"So you do understand a little of the law. You should also be acutely aware that you are on the wrong side of it. I'll tell you, maybe. It would take a hundred-year conviction to ten years. I'm not sure I'm willing to do that because you violated good people with full intention for them to be in comas for the rest of their lives. I'm not good with that."

The male was looking for anything to lighten his sentence. He started to sing. "We were paid by Moniken Gravenhole after getting our targets from her and to her. One-quarter up front and the rest upon delivery."

Rivka looked at Chaz, who nodded almost imperceptibly.

"How did she pay you?" Rivka asked.

"Credit transfer to our hidden account."

"I'm going to need that number." Rivka smiled pleasantly. The female became frantic, kicking and trying to claw. Red body-slammed her into the table before holding her up once more. "You won't be able to use that money, and we'll find it anyway as we'll backtrack your whereabouts until we come across the account. Then I'll issue a warrant, and we'll take it all. Right now, I only want to use it to backtrack the payment."

"Fine," the male conceded, then recited the memorized number. Between Clevarious, Chaz, and Dennicron, Rivka had no need to write anything down. She knew they would be digging into the system to find the trail within seconds.

"A password would save us time," Dennicron said. He gave it to her. The SIs continued their search. "Got it."

Chaz and Dennicron looked at each other, beaming. Rivka rolled her finger. Dennicron bowed her head to Chaz.

He brought up the holoscreen over the conference table. "Payment received from Moniken Gravenhole, who doesn't exist, and her shell company, Graven Enterprises, which also exists only on paper. They were formed by Graveyard Industries, another shell corporation that is owned by another corporation that is not a shell. Korantall United."

"As in, owned by Koranta Delaveen," Rivka posited.

"Sister of the ambassador *and* second wife of one Ambassador Bik Tia Nor."

"The ambassadors keep their knobby paws clean. Top cover and ground cover." Rivka looked at the Furlorians. The male looked back, hope in his big cat eyes. "Sentences to serve concurrently. Ten years for both of you."

He exhaled hard and turned to his sister. She was not as enamored of a ten-year sentence as he was. "Life down to ten years. Our contacts will be long gone by the time we get out," the male said.

Rivka agreed. "I will dismantle that organization in such a way that the pieces will never be able to reassemble. You have a warrior who is still head over heels in love with you. I'm putting you in the brig on Tyrosint with further transfer to work-release on the planet. They need good workers, and it's completely voluntary, but I expect your race prefers open spaces so you can run and feel free."

"Isn't that a bit racist?" the male asked.

"Is my presumption incorrect?"

"No. Outside under a sun and a blue sky sounds pretty good right about now. For what it's worth, I'm sorry, Magistrate. We were looking at taking our riches and going to Verdance, an agricultural planet. All the while, we were ignoring the people we were hurting. I'll serve my time. I deserve it. My sister went along with me because I'm the big brother. That's how it is with our people. Maybe she can serve a lesser sentence."

"If I had put you in Jhiordaan, you wouldn't be the same because they would break you. After Tyrosint, maybe you'll be better. Return to the brig. We'll deliver you to the station before the day ends. Ten years. Both of you."

The male thanked Rivka while the female glared. Rivka stared back until the Furlorian blinked, her spirit finally surrendering to the consequences of her decisions.

"Bring me that doctor."

"With pleasure." Red, Chaz, and Dennicron returned the Furlorians to the brig and yanked the doctor out of the room. He tried to fall down, refusing to walk. Red picked him up by the back of his pants and propelled him forward, slamming his head into the door to the conference room to open it. He thrust the man inside and propped him up. "He was a bit uncooperative, Magistrate."

"Do you not care how much time you'll serve?"

"I'm just a doctor."

"You're a criminal. Certified bottom feeder. You tried to take people's lives, and that is a crime against sentience. Give me your hand."

Red shoved the doctor's hand forward. Rivka took it

before he could snatch it back. "Why were you stealing blood?"

The man looked frantically for a way out. *Panic. He was caught. Deny!*

"I'm just a doctor. I do what I'm told."

"Give us your bank information to confirm you get normal pay for normal doctor duties."

"No…" He shook his head, looking for a way out, but in his mind, he contemplated his account number and the bank. Rivka recited it aloud.

"Hey! That's my account number."

"Lucky guess," Rivka replied and let go of the man's hand. She knew exactly what they were going to find. A massive deposit, about a year's worth of a doctor's normal salary as a hiring bonus.

Chaz replied. "Fifty thousand credits paid by Graven Enterprises."

"You're dirty," Rivka announced.

"I didn't know they were bad! I did nothing wrong," he pleaded in a whining voice.

"Putting healthy people into comas so you can take their blood is good doctoring?"

"They were volunteers on a deep-space study!" he declared hopefully.

"We both know that isn't true since Private Elbinar was brought to you already in a coma. I don't know about the others, but I only need to know for sure about Elbinar. Unlawful detention, theft, and the worst charge, crime against sentience. I'm suspending your license to practice and notifying the medical board with a recommendation to revoke it. They can take their time since you'll be on

Jhiordaan, serving twenty years for theft of blood and an additional thirty-five years for crime against sentience. To serve sequentially. That's more than fifty years, Doctor. I'm confiscating your ill-gotten gains. Congratulations. You're broke, without a license, and ready to spend the next half of your life in prison."

"That sucks," he managed to say.

"Is that the best you have? You're lucky I don't toss you out an airlock. You are a despicable creature. If I never see you again, that will be too soon." Rivka raised her chin. Red took her meaning and yanked the doctor backward and dragged him down the corridor to toss him into the brig.

"We have the documentation sorted and money transferred from both accounts into the Magistrates' holding account," Chaz reported. "We've submitted the accounting data to the High Chancellor's office."

Rivka acknowledged the quick work. She pointed to the hologrid area above the table, and Chaz projected the financial reports.

Tyler, how much longer? I'm itching to catch some big-time scumbags.

On our way back because they had everything under control. This nurse is good.

"Lieutenant Edwin, Rivka here. The nurse in the medical bay is free to go, free to move on. She helped us and is a victim in this, just like the six people getting pumped dry."

"One person," the lieutenant's voice projected over the room's speakers. "The other five are complaining that they have contracts to donate their blood at the price of keeping them out of sight for ten years and building their cash pile."

"That's one of the most fucked-up things I've ever heard," Rivka replied.

"Can they sign away their blood and life like that?" the lieutenant asked.

Rivka had been thinking about it and didn't like the answer. "They can. One victim and five who were misled and taken for a ride. Turn them loose to go their own way. I think Tyrosint is looking for more agro workers. They'd be off the grid down there. Sell it, Edwin. They get to live while officially hiding. If I need to put them into witness protection, I can sign an order for that, too, but they have to comply with the law. If they break the law, they lose their support."

"Maybe it'd be best if you talked with them. I'm not very good at making civilians feel comfortable. Maybe your guy, the tall, lanky, and weird one?"

"You can do this, Lieutenant. Welcome to being an officer. Put your best foot forward and save their lives. It's what the Bad Company is good at. Tell Elbinar the Furlorian will be on Tyrosint and then on work-release on the planet in case he wishes to pursue an ill-advised relationship."

Edwin laughed loud and long. "Those are the only relationships we pursue, Magistrate. It was a pleasure working with you. Next time, try not to leave us any dead bodies. Bad Company out."

Rivka looked at the financials, and the numbers reminded her. "Come clean, you knuckleheads. Did you certify running?"

"Yes. Running to the bay after the security-bot ambush," Chaz said.

"But no blood, which is odd on a case to dismantle the blood trade. Arrest, swearing?"

"You bagged the Ambassador first, and during that arrest, there was a planetwide carpet-bombing of profanity."

"There was not. You were there!"

"I was, but my story is better."

"These are real people betting real money. Don't make shit up." Rivka pointed the finger of shame at Red and brushed it.

"You only went on a tirade after the trial."

"I was pretty mad."

"That's when we'll call it, Magistrate, but I think you'll get to arrest the ambassador again, along with the Foromme ambassador and his sister."

"I like that. Let's pack 'em and stack 'em, then rack 'em and jack 'em. C, get us out of here as soon as everyone's on board. First stop, the station, then Foromme and one Koranta Delaveen."

"What if she fights back?" Red wondered.

"They always fight back, but not for very long." She winked at him. "I'm catching a shower. Chaz, transmit the holding order for those three. The doctor is awaiting prison transport, and the Furlorians are assigned to Tyrosint's brig until further notice with work-release to the planet at the head of station's discretion. The five who were under contract are now under my protection and to be sent to the planet under fake identities to work agricultural support. And Chaz, find me Koranta Delaveen."

CHAPTER TWENTY-ONE

Wyatt Earp, **in Orbit over Foromme**

"Is there any hope that they'll let us land?" Rivka asked.

"Their process seems convoluted, to say the least," Clevarious replied.

"Time to pull out the big hammer. Get me Landing Control, please."

The next sound was the voice of an angry controller.

"We're swamped, and you didn't pre-register. You have to wait until there's an opening."

"I'm sorry, but I'm in pursuit of a Federation suspect charged with crimes against sentience. Is the planet of Foromme shielding this individual?"

"No, but you have to wait your turn. I only handle the spatial awareness."

"Under Federation Laws, Appendix D, Chapter Seven, I am exercising my right as a Federation Diplomat to jump to the head of the line. I have your name and number to figure prominently, and heaven help you if your delay resulted in the suspect getting away. You said you handle all ships traveling from the surface? Shut that down. No one leaves Foromme until the suspect is in custody."

"I can only do that with orders from my superiors. I can move you to the front of the line, but that's the best I can do."

"Thank you. I'm contacting your superiors immediately." Rivka waited for the line to close and *Wyatt Earp* to skip past the array of ships trapped in orbit. "Clevarious, get me the chancellor's office, please."

The SI replied immediately. "They say that the chancellor is busy and to leave a message."

"Tell them we request immediate restriction of all travel to orbit until our suspect is in custody. Crimes against sentience, and Foromme leadership does not want to be seen as shielding this individual. Send that to the chancellor's office and everyone else in the chain from that person to the controller I just talked with. Take us in and drop us on Koranta's estate. We go in fully armed."

Rivka hurried to her quarters and dressed. Tyler shook his head. "This is the hardest part," he said. "I don't know if you'll come back."

"I always come back because I'm surrounded by good people and I keep my wits about me. Koranta will come once her support collapses. We're freezing all her accounts the instant we appear in the air over her home. I'm going to transmit a message to Lance Reynolds too, letting him know that both Foromme and Delegor are involved in this and may be spearheading it. We'll know when we grab her and her records."

Tyler waved his hands at her. "I don't care about any of

that. I wish there was a different way to secure your suspect and have her brought to you. Do you have to go?"

"I do. There are things one sees and hears that aren't replicable in the sanitary environment of an interview room. And I train for this. There's a lot to be said for being the judge, but I'm my own investigator, too. Going in comes with the territory. I'll come home. I'm not going to end my short life on a planet like Foromme. If you wonder, the reason I didn't involve the locals is I don't want to give them a chance to show their true colors. I have no intention of arresting the whole planet. Not today, anyway." She winked at him and finished putting on her ballistic protection. Head to toe, combat boots and helmet included.

Rivka left her Magistrate's jacket on her chair. It wouldn't fit over her gear. She made sure the Magistrate's logo was visible and headed for the cargo bay, where she met Red, Lindy, Chaz, and Dennicron. Cole had a powered combat suit on the deck and was climbing in.

"Hang on." The Magistrate closed on him.

"Just doing my job, ma'am."

Red raised an eyebrow.

"Destroy any weapons emplacements that fire on us unless you can destroy them without collateral damage before they fire," Rivka explained.

"I can do that." Cole entered the suit, buttoned up, and ran through the start-up sequence.

"Good," Red offered. "Rich bad guys always have real firepower protecting their empires."

"So do we." Rivka hoisted her railgun and checked it quickly to make sure she had a full load, full power, and it was clean and ready to fire. She knew Red had done that already, but where weapons were involved, it was everyone's individual responsibility to double- and triple-check.

She also had her neutron pulse weapon, but that was tucked inside the bulletproof outerwear.

Wyatt Earp swept toward the city from the outskirts, but Koranta lived close to the city center, not optimal from the viewpoint of a raid. There were too many egress routes into the neighborhood where collateral damage was too high.

"If she gets out of the compound, then we're screwed, and we'll have to get local support. Chaz, are her accounts locked?"

"They are, from Korantall United to her private accounts to the servants' slush fund. No one is going to see a single credit from her until we unlock the accounts," the SI confirmed.

"Servant slush fund…" Rivka murmured. "Insert parameters?"

Clevarious replied, *The closest I can get you is the roof access of the main building. You'll be able to jump from the roof to the ground to secure the three visible exits. I'll hold the ship over the main building as close as possible. The best we can gauge is that she's somewhere inside. And if there's an escape tunnel, all bets are off.*

"Is there any way we can scan the area below the surface, looking for such things?"

Of course, but in a busy metropolitan city, I'm sure it will look like a spaghetti maze down there.

"Give it a try, and we'll secure the surface-level doorways and work our way through the building." Rivka looked from face to face. "Cole, you first. Skip the rooftop and jump straight into the courtyard."

A mini-bark signaled the arrival of Tiny Man Titan.

"Keep him away from the opening," Cole said, using his suit's external speakers.

Clodagh stood there holding the baby, with the dog-like alien at her feet. She waved, received Cole's salute, and went back into the ship. "I'll be on the bridge," she shouted over her shoulder.

"The family that fights together stays together," Red said.

"Kick ass to make it last," Lindy offered.

"Kick it to get it." Rivka shrugged.

"How warped are we that going into a fight is an aphrodisiac?" Lindy asked.

Rivka stayed still to avoid looking like she agreed or disagreed.

"Would we be here if we weren't a little warped?" Red replied. "No better job in the 'verse." He leaned over the cargo ramp. "Get ready, Cole. Looks like we're getting close."

Red is correct, Clevarious confirmed. *On my mark, Private Cole. Mark.*

Cole took three oversized steps and was gone, dropping a hundred meters toward a smooth courtyard surrounding a fountain. No vehicles were present.

He activated his jets and touched down softly. *Wyatt Earp* maneuvered toward the roof of the main building. The outbuildings were small, little more than decoration since the mansion dominated the compound that took up a full quarter of a block in the middle of the high-rent district.

The ship descended to a point where the ramp barely overlapped the roof since *Wyatt Earp* was a big ship and other buildings were close.

Red gave his war cry and ran out the back. The rest followed, with Lindy jumping last after making sure the Magistrate made it. As *Wyatt Earp* started moving away, Sahved flung himself from the ramp, bicycling his legs and waving his arms until he landed on the rooftop, where he stopped his wild gyrations. The ship moved ten meters away, centering over the compound to get the most breathing room.

The rooftop was flat, without immediately visible access from inside. Red pointed at the three sides where the doors were located. "Go, go, go!" He took his position and waved at the Magistrate. Chaz grabbed Sahved and Dennicron went with Lindy. As soon as they reached the edge, they went over.

Rivka braced herself for the impact, deciding to hit and roll. That saved her ankles, but her shoulder hit harder than she wanted. Her ballistic protection protected her body from serious injury. Red grunted on impact but remained upright. He limped the first couple of steps toward the door before shrugging off the injury.

Red reached the door. "Easy way or hard way?"

"Try the easy way—a gentle knock. I have my creds in hand," Rivka replied.

Prepare to breach on my mark, Red announced to the team. *Any defenses, Cole?*

None that I can see. Looks clear. Sensors show seven bodies.

Four on the first floor and three on the second. No one on the third.

Red pounded on the door with his meat-mallet fist.

Rivka tried to get close, but he kept her from getting right in front of the door.

Someone is coming to answer the door. I don't see any weapons on the scan.

Thanks, Cole, Rivka replied.

The door opened slowly, and a Foromme face peered out. The servant tried to close the door, but Red blocked them.

In the back of her mind, she heard Cole giving instructions regarding the layout to the other two breach teams, with directions for Lindy and Dennicron to hit the steps to the right of their door and head upstairs.

"I am Magistrate Rivka Anoa." She held her creds before her, stepping close to show them clearly to the person who'd answered the door. "I have a warrant for the arrest of Koranta Delaveen. Where is she?"

The servant shook her head and mumbled.

"I guess it's the hard way, then."

Go, go, go! Red called.

Dennicron destroyed the door in front of her, rushed through, took a hard right, and headed upstairs, with Lindy close on her heels.

Chaz burst through their door and ran in, looking for where the people were, as Cole had described.

Rivka pushed her way inside. "Get outside," she ordered the servant. Red gave the individual a hearty push toward the open door.

Two are heading down the stairs toward the basement. Straight ahead, first left.

Rivka ran before Red could stop her. She hit the door and kept going. "Stop!" she shouted down the well-lit stairs after catching a glimpse of a male turning the corner ahead.

"Wait up," Red called after her, taking the steps three at a time on the way down. Rivka accelerated, staying out of her bodyguard's reach. All he could do was keep running.

At the next corner, they found a series of rooms and corridors. Rivka slowed. *Cole?*

Straight ahead, left, then right. Rivka hit the left at full speed, bouncing off the wall to keep her moving forward. She did the same at the right turn and caught the male servant. She grabbed his collar and dragged him down backward.

Rivka vaulted him and kept running. The person she knew to be Koranta was trying to close and secure the door ahead.

The Magistrate had the scent and was on her final approach. She hit the door with her shoulder, bending it but not breaking through. She staggered to the side as Red hit it with his weight and power. It screamed as the deadbolt ripped away from the frame. He stumbled through.

A flash and the boom of a slugthrower. The round slammed into Rivka's chest, bending her over backward. A second shot went over her head. Red fired once from the floor.

"No!" Rivka cried before she toppled over backward. She tried to stand, but the pain in her chest was too great.

"She had a cannon pointed at my head, Magistrate," Red replied softly. "I'm sorry. I could not let her take the shot."

He stood, checked the body, and returned to help Rivka up.

"Is she?" Rivka wondered.

"Yeah. She succumbed to her wounds."

Rivka peeked past Red to find a massive hole blown through Koranta's chest. A railgun at point-blank range did significant damage. Red secured her weapon, taking it as evidence.

"This isn't going to go over well," Rivka said. She walked away, looking for the individual who had been running with Koranta.

She found him outside with the other five from the household and walked up to him. "Where were you two going?"

"Why don't you ask the mistress?"

"Because I'm asking you," Rivka countered, leaning close to touch his shoulder. He looked at her hand before continuing. "It's not my place to say."

In his mind, he saw the escape tunnel. He didn't know anything beyond that.

"Where does the escape tunnel lead?"

"She got away!" He cheered before making a gesture she assumed was rude on Foromme.

"Almost," Rivka replied. "Who here knows about her role in the blood trade?"

They remained stone-faced and silent. She walked down the line, whispering "blood trade" as she passed each. None of them knew anything about it. Koranta had treated them well, and they guarded her secrets.

The other four of the Magistrate's team were still in the house. *We'll need anything related to her businesses,* Rivka requested.

Her computer system is thumbprint-activated, Chaz replied.

She's in the basement. Down the stairs in the middle of the house, down the corridor, left, then right. You can get her print there.

"How do we get to the roof?" Rivka asked.

One of the servants didn't think the information was critical. "Up the main staircase to the third floor. There's a door on the top landing. The steps to the roof are inside."

Local authorities are on their way, Clodagh reported from the ship.

This could have gone a lot better, but I've found that big-league criminals don't like being taken alive.

Rivka strolled to the front of the compound to open the gates, swinging them wide. She directed Cole to move the servants to the side while the others continued searching the house to recover any evidence they could gather that would allow her to either tie up the investigation and close the case or lead her deeper into the trade.

The first three vehicles came screaming into the compound's circular drive. The law enforcement officers jumped out and took positions behind the vehicles, aiming at Rivka. Red pushed her behind him.

Cole encouraged them to put their weapons away by using his jets to fly above their heads, then he landed in the middle of the group. Someone fired, but the round bounced off harmlessly.

"This is Magistrate Rivka Anoa from the Federation. We're here under orders from General Lance Reynolds to dismantle the blood trade. The owner of this home has been implicated. We are here under Federation orders and laws. Put your weapons down." Cole looked from face to face until they complied, not because of the power of his argument but because they couldn't fight him.

Rivka hurried into the silence, holding her creds in front of her.

The one in charge moved to the front and ripped the creds from Rivka's hand. "You'll want to take care with those," she warned. He tried to keep her credentials. "Please give them back."

He stuffed them into his pocket. Red seized the officer and lifted him so Rivka could take back what was hers. When she had what she wanted, Red put the man down.

"You'll pay for that," he snarled.

"What do you know about Koranta Delaveen?"

"The Delaveens are highly respected on Foromme. Where is Koranta?" the man asked pointedly.

"She shot at me and didn't survive the shootout," Rivka replied.

"You murdered her?" The officer removed his hat, groaning and stamping his foot.

"This is why you weren't informed of my raid on her compound. She was accused of crimes against sentience, which carries the death penalty in the Federation. It appears she would have received a great deal of official protection rather than letting the legal system do its job."

"You didn't have to kill her. What was the rush in getting her?"

"My orders were to eliminate the blood trade. I believe that I have now done that. Koranta Delaveen took people's lives from them for vanity's sake alone. It's a shame that she went down that road, don't you think?"

"She did no such thing."

"You mean to say you're embarrassed that such crimes were taking place under your nose. Anything else could be construed as being complicit in her crimes. What did you know about her shell corporations and the buying of blood?" Rivka reached for him, but he stayed farther than arm's length from her.

"Nothing. The Delaveens are philanthropists, always giving. This isn't going to sit well, not well at all."

"I expect you're right about that. Red, get a body bag and collect the remains for transfer to *Wyatt Earp*. We'll return them once we're done with the examination."

"I wouldn't do that."

Rivka glared at him until he backed away. Above them, *Wyatt Earp* moved close to the rooftop. A bag fluttered out the back and out of sight.

On it, Lindy said. *Sahved is searching. He's already found three hand-written ledgers that were hidden.*

The Yemilorian appeared on the rooftop and jumped into the ship. He was gone for a few seconds before hopping back to the roof.

Give official notification to the Federation, Clevarious, regarding the demise of Mrs. Delaveen. Connect me with the General, please.

Rivka walked into the house while Red took a position in the doorway to keep anyone from following.

Rivka, Lance Reynolds answered. *Tell me you have good news.*

Let me start with the good news. I believe that we have

broken the back of the blood trade. We've recovered all kidnapped parties and stopped the supply side of the chain. We discovered the one behind the orchestration of it, but she was killed before we could ask her any questions.

Sounds like good news, mostly. Are you able to access her personal logs or anything like that?

We're doing that right now, taking her computer systems and personal journals. We'll find out if there are any others involved. Now to the bad news. She's Koranta Delaveen, the sister of Ambassador Delaveen of Foromme, and it gets worse. She's the wife of Ambassador Bik Tia Nor of Delegor.

The General didn't speak for the longest time. She thought the connection had been lost, but in case it hadn't, she waited.

That is *bad. I'll have to do some damage control from this end, but you are positive it was her?*

I am. We have a solid link from her to the ones who kidnapped the warriors. I know the Bad Company is a private enterprise, but is there anyone in the main halls who would keep tabs on them and report to the Federation Council, as in, would the ambassadors be able to learn enough to target Bad Company personnel with some precision? The kidnappers seemed to know where the warriors were going on vacation. They were waiting for them.

I'll look into it. I've called the ambassadors into my office. I'll inform them of Koranta's death. Maybe you should look at leaving Foromme sooner rather than later, the General advised.

I think that's exactly what we'll do once we have what we came here for. We'll return straight to Yoll and report our findings. I'll make my report directly to the High Chancellor.

Perfect. Good work taking down the blood trade. That is an abomination, and it makes me want to rip off their heads and shit down their necks. Unfortunately, I don't get to do that anymore, so I'll be kind, but I'll be watching, too. They are both recipients of the blood. That tells me they were knee-deep in it. I'll let you know if I find anything.

Rivka returned to the front door but didn't go outside. "They brought reinforcements," Red whispered over his shoulder.

Time to go, people. Wrap up what you're doing and go back to the ship. Cover us, Cole. You'll be last on board.

Rivka found the steps and headed up. Red waited until the others were climbing. He followed Lindy up, carrying the body bag. They hit the roof fast and ran across and up the ramp into the ship. Cole flew from the courtyard to the roof, where he landed and ran across and into the cargo bay.

The ship nosed upward as the cargo ramp was closing and raced for space. The second it cleared the atmosphere, the Gate formed, and they were through. Once they reached Yollin space, they slowly merged into the normal traffic pattern. The Magistrate needed time to compile the information, and most importantly, to think.

CHAPTER TWENTY-TWO

***Wyatt Earp*, in Orbit over Yoll**

"Hurry up," Rivka muttered, waiting for the report from Chaz and Dennicron on what they had found in the computer systems. She thumbed through the notebooks. One had dates and transactions. The amounts were listed in ccs, which Rivka translated as cubic centimeters. She had both her husband and brother listed if the initials were anything to go by. It all tied together with the clinic name where one BTN was to receive two hundred ccs on the date Rivka and Chaz had found the ambassador there, getting that exact amount of enhanced blood. It cracked the code, and the dominos fell.

Since her husband and brother didn't pay, they didn't leave a money trail. She charged everyone else vast sums, and that funded the operation. Thanks to the enhancements, they were draining five hundred cubic centimeters of blood every two weeks. With four donors? That would be a thousand ccs every week. She was going to grow richer than she was and even more powerful as the ability to get enhanced reached a broader sector of the galaxy's population.

Those who could afford ten thousand credits for each one hundred ccs, with tips welcomed to improve a person's place on the waiting list.

The SIs had yet to crack the final account, the one into which the money poured, since it was hidden behind numerous barriers. It was the type of account rich people used to hide their money from all comers, legal entities and criminals alike.

The disturbing part in the journal was the initials she couldn't identify, but she had a team of investigators to dig into it.

Sahved showed that he was a quality addition to the team. Chaz and Dennicron continued their assistance, which transcended a normal person's capabilities, but could they make the hard decisions in the right way? She wasn't yet sure. She needed to continue their training.

And a new family on board. While she waited for the SIs, she found Clodagh, Cole, and the baby in their quarters.

"Just checking in. How is our newest addition to the team?"

"The fast growth is moving her through the process a little more quickly than other babies. We've all heard the horror stories, but not so much here. We're already at a single block of sleep that lasts six hours. We just got up, and I feel like a normal human being versus the always-tired look of other new mothers."

"And Cole, no more undercover operations for you. Nothing personal."

"I'm happy to hear that. It was not my thing, Magistrate. Thanks for trusting me, but coming to with half my blood missing was no way to wake up. I'd rather wake up to a baby crying."

Clodagh's mouth fell open. "That's your comparison? Getting drained to death or a baby crying?"

Cole regrouped quickly for his counterattack. He held his fingers a few millimeters apart. "Those two are not this far apart," he spread his arms all the way, "but this far apart. Opposite ends of the spectrum."

"Uh-huh." Clodagh wasn't convinced, but she got over it the instant he hugged her and the baby.

"What's her name?" Rivka asked.

"We've decided on Alana Siobhan Cole."

"So let it be written. So let it be done. I'll notify the Singularity." Rivka hesitated. "That's Irish, isn't it? So it's not spelled how it sounds. S-h-e-V-O-N."

Clodagh laughed. "No." She spelled it. Rivka frowned.

"Have it your way." Rivka left them alone and found Chaz and Dennicron in the corridor.

"Tell me good news."

"The universe's rate of expansion remains constant," Chaz replied.

"Is that supposed to be good? Never mind. Tell me you cracked the accounts. We're going to have to go planetside pretty soon, and I want to stuff that candle into the top of this cake."

"We have not, and I'm afraid to inform you that we will probably not be able to. Despite having the body on board, none of the biometrics work to access the system. None of the usual digital accesses are finding any traction. This is an encryption that we've not seen before."

"But we know the account. We can't just look into it?"

"Correct."

"Is it locked down, at least?"

"It is by your order that we've transmitted to the financial institution, which is reputable."

"Then that is one of those things that will have to languish until such time as the bank gives us access."

"That's just it. They don't have access either. It's a completely secure account."

"As long as they can keep credits from leaving it and going into it, then we'll make do without the totals. Analyze the rest of her spending and see if there was a reduction in what she used to spend. Maybe we can guesstimate the amount she's covering from her illicit operation because I'm betting she never reduced her spending, only changed where the money was coming from."

The SIs nodded vigorously and hurried away, leaving Rivka to her thoughts. She sauntered to the bridge so she could look at the view from the front of the ship.

After a minute of peace, Ryleigh spoke from the pilot's station. "Magistrate, we're cleared to land."

Rivka reluctantly climbed out of the captain's seat. "I'm sorry we weren't able to spend more time on Tyrosint Station. You three seemed to have a good time there."

Ryleigh talked over her shoulder as she guided the ship into the landing pattern. "What do you mean? You think we like being the center of attention from hot guys in uniform?"

Rivka attempted an answer. "Yes?"

"Okay. We do."

"Once we're done here, set course for Tyrosint Station. We could all use some shore leave, and if I'm going to send people to the planet for rehab, I probably need to see what it's like first."

Rivka headed to her quarters to get her Magistrate's jacket. She ran into Joseph and Petricia coming from the galley.

"Are we going to talk about what happened on those ships?"

"I don't think so," Joseph said. "You don't need anything more than you already know. Punish me if you must, but I regret nothing and will change nothing in my coming years."

"Punishment is to stop a repeat of a behavior. I don't think there's anything we need to change. There were bad people whose only remorse was that they got caught. One should have more of a conscience than that. You left them alive to live with the remorse they *should* feel."

"We'll go with that." Joseph smiled. Petricia nodded with a slight movement.

"I'm sorry for putting you in harm's way."

Joseph tsk-tsked her apology. "I'm an old man. If I'm in harm's way, it's because I put myself there. I apologize to Petricia for bringing her into the consequences of my poor judgment. But we recovered well because of good friends who will stop at nothing to save their own."

The ship shuddered as it bumped through the upper atmosphere.

Rivka rested her hand on his shoulder. "Thank you.

Now, *we* have to see the High Chancellor. Be ready to go in fifteen if you wouldn't mind."

High Chancellor's Office, The Royal City of Khn'Chik on Yoll

"That's what you have?" High Chancellor Wyatt reviewed the evidence that the team had compiled on the short trip between Foromme and Yoll. She thanked the gods for Chaz, Dennicron, and Clevarious.

The High Chancellor had not allowed any of the support team into his office. Red, Lindy, Sahved, the SCAMPs, Joseph, and Petricia waited in the outer office. She had thought she was going to get her ass chewed. She felt like a screw-up. This case hadn't gone how she wanted.

Wyatt watched her. "What were your expectations?"

"Roll up the organization from bottom to top, catch the bad guy, and parade through the streets with the vile scum."

"A little dramatic, but I see. What *didn't* you accomplish?" Wyatt pressed.

"I don't understand. We killed the perp."

"You knew she was guilty beyond a shadow of a doubt?"

"Beyond a shadow of a doubt. It made too much sense when the final arrows pointed at her. And if Red hadn't killed her, she would have killed him. The gun was military-grade, not for civilian sale or use."

"That doesn't point to any more or less guilt when it comes to the blood trade."

"No, but she was a lot younger than she should have

been. Initial indications from the autopsy show she had Elbinar's nanocytes in her, too."

"She was a user. Maybe she established the trade to serve her and her family." Wyatt leaned back and crossed his arms. For him, this was a casual conversation. For Rivka, it was the stake of self-doubt driven into her heart, creating a chasm that cut to her very soul.

"It's not a crime to be a user or addicted, but that changes the depth of the crimes against sentience. I judged her and punished her for the same thing that her husband claimed. The nature of her being was on trial. She was relentlessly driven to get ahead and stay ahead. The Delaveen family had money when the latest were born, but the ambassador and his sister sent the value of what they had into the stratosphere."

"The nature of success," Wyatt replied. "Does that give one carte blanche to trample on the rights of others?"

"Of course not." Rivka was certain of that. "If someone's nature is being a criminal, then they will remain at odds with society for all their days. Incarceration until rehabilitation is achieved. If rehab isn't possible, then they need to remain separated from law-abiding citizens."

"The nature of their being will always be a touchy subject, and when used as a defense, must be given due consideration. However, crimes are crimes. Committing one while under the influence does not relieve one of their responsibility, but rehabilitation could be accomplished through getting clean. It may not take long. Isn't our job to eliminate recidivists?"

"Death sentence for every crime would do that, but that's not the right answer." Rivka shook her head and held her hand up to forestall a snappy answer. "Punishment appropriate to the crime. Did Koranta Delaveen deserve to die?"

"According to Red's statement, she was aiming the 'cannon,' his word, at his head. She had already shot at you twice, and you were down. Red didn't know if you had survived the attack. He made the decision to save his life. I find no fault in his actions. I think that's when Red declared blood. I think a bone bruise counts."

"Thanks for that, High Chancellor. He wasn't proud of what he'd done. He had gone down when the door opened after using his body as a battering ram. He said he should have shot the door apart."

"That would have killed whoever was behind it. You were carrying your usual if I'm not mistaken." Rivka nodded. "And she was trying to get away. Time was of the essence. And then she fired first. Twice. Had you not been in your body armor, this would be a conversation with the rest of your team because you'd be dead."

"My team would make me sound like a hero." Rivka smiled weakly. The High Chancellor strolled to a side table and poured Rivka a glass from a decanter. He poured himself one, too.

He offered her the glass and held it up. "Here's to getting our people back and solving the crime."

"Yes, sir," she said woodenly. "I feel like we could have done something differently."

"Your problem is that those running the operation are already trying to cause trouble for you. Important government officials who are criminals are no longer important government officials. General Reynolds had an interesting conversation with the two ambassadors, who seemed much more angry than distraught. You have the confidence of this government. You have nothing to worry about. You did as well as anyone could do in what was a crappy situation. You were set up to fail, chasing those who were directly involved. We should have pulled those two ambassadors aside and given them the third degree until they cracked."

"That would have helped."

"But we didn't know," Wyatt countered, stopping Rivka's second-guessing cold. "We didn't know until you found the other facts in the case. Most importantly, Private Elbinar."

"And we recovered our own people, too. The Furlorians should have never been able to snatch them, but they were good."

"Indeed. I hear you have a new addition to your team. I thought Clodagh wasn't due for a few more months? Why did the baby come early?"

"It seems no one told us that enhanced people create enhanced babies who can't be bothered with the usual gestation period. The baby will grow at least twice as fast, too."

"Good luck with that menagerie on board your ship," Wyatt told her.

"I wouldn't have it any other way."

"Bring your people inside. I want to thank them personally." Wyatt waved at the door. Rivka hurried to open it so her team could join her.

They filed in, Red first since he'd been leaning against the door and almost fell through when Rivka opened it.

Wyatt greeted them one by one with a personal comment for each until Joseph reached him, when he stopped cold. Joseph took Wyatt by the shoulders and stared into his eyes. The two men stayed that way for a long time before they smiled and hugged.

Joseph spoke first. "I wondered where you'd gotten off to, little brother."

THE END
JUDGE, JURY, & EXECUTIONER, BOOK 12

If you like this book, please leave a review. I love reviews since they tell other readers that this book is worth their time and money. I hope you feel that way now that you've finished the latest installment. Please drop me a line and let me know you like Rivka's adventures and want them to continue. This is my new favorite series. I hope you agree.

Don't stop now! Keep turning the pages as Craig hits his *Author Notes* with thoughts about this book and the good stuff that happens in the *Kurtherian Gambit* Universe.

Your favorite legal eagle will return! I guarantee it:).

Back in the saddle of the *Judge, Jury, & Executioner*. Here we have book twelve, which revisits a theme from a long, long time ago.

Any time someone has something another covets, they will take unnatural actions to satisfy their greed.

Thank goodness we have someone like Rivka to take a personal interest in resolving this issue, but there will always be envy and greed. It's resolved for now, which is the best anyone can do.

I brought back Joseph and Petricia, too. They had seen little action since the *Nomad* days and needed to find their groove. So they joined Rivka on this case, and it didn't go as they had hoped. But the loyalty of good friends cannot be undervalued or understated.

Rivka would go to the ends of the universe to rescue her people.

Here in Alaska, which seems like it's on the edge of the

universe, it's getting light fast and is completely dark for only about four hours a night. By the time this book publishes, we'll be close to twenty-four hours of daylight, and we'll stay that way for nearly three months.

We're getting another dog—Stanley, a six-year-old pit bull, is coming to us. That took an act of Congress, but thanks to a great pet transport company who left no stone unturned, looks like we'll get him on May 28. We have to drive to Anchorage, six or seven hours away, and meet him at the airport. Then we'll spend the night before coming home.

I have my treadmill and was pounding out some miles with that by the time the weather warmed up. We've had highs in the forties and fifties (Fahrenheit) for the past week, and that is melting up a storm. We're doing plenty of walking outside nowadays. I'm feeling better about my body. I still have a lot of weight to lose. I have lung damage, so the extra twenty pounds are tough to haul around. Anything I can lose benefits me. Walking is my key—burn the calories. I cut out processed sugar a couple of years ago since I don't want to get diabetes like my mom, my sister, and my brother. My mom and brother aren't even heavy, but they got it all the same.

Next books in the queue are the final books in the *Battleship: Leviathan* series, which isn't in the Kurtherian Gambit universe. Then I think I'll jam out *A Fatal Bragg*, the fourth book in the Ian Bragg Thriller series to keep life in that series, and then JJE13—*The Interview*. I hope you like that one. I've already had a good discussion with my insider team about how that story will flow, and they were excited about it. I think you'll like it, too. Coming fall of 2021.

Peace, fellow humans.

Please join my Newsletter (craigmartelle.com—please, please, please sign up!), or you can follow me on Facebook.

If you liked this story, you might like some of my other books. You can join my mailing list by dropping by my website www.craigmartelle.com or if you have any comments, shoot me a note at craig@craigmartelle.com. I am always happy to hear from people who've read my work. I try to answer every email I receive.

If you liked the story, please write a short review for me on Amazon. I greatly appreciate any kind words; even one or two sentences go a long way. The number of reviews an eBook receives greatly improves how well an eBook does on Amazon.

Amazon – www.amazon.com/author/craigmartelle

BookBub – https://www.bookbub.com/authors/craig-martelle

Facebook – www.facebook.com/authorcraigmartelle

My web page – https://craigmartelle.com

That's it—break's over, back to writing the next book.

The Expanding Universe—science fiction anthologies

Krimson Empire (co-written with Julia Huni)—a galactic race for justice

Zenophobia (#)—a space archaeological adventure

End Times Alaska (#)—a Permuted Press publication—a post-apocalyptic survivalist adventure

Nightwalker (a Frank Roderus series)—A post-apocalyptic western adventure

End Days (#) (co-written with E.E. Isherwood)—a post-apocalyptic adventure

Successful Indie Author (#)—a non-fiction series to help self-published authors

Monster Case Files (co-written with Kathryn Hearst)—A Warner twins mystery adventure

Rick Banik (#)—Spy & terrorism action adventure

Ian Bragg Thrillers—a man with a conscience who kills bad guys for money

Published exclusively by Craig Martelle, Inc

The Dragon's Call by Angelique Anderson & Craig A. Price, Jr.—an epic fantasy quest

A Couples Travel—a non-fiction travel series

For a complete list of Craig's books, stop by his website —https://craigmartelle.com